BETTING ON US

A WILDE LOVE NOVEL

KELLY COLLINS

BOOK NOOK PRESS

Copyright © 2018 by Kelly Collins

No part of this publication may be reproduced, distributed, or transmitted in any form or by any means, including photocopying, recording, or other electronic or mechanical methods, without the prior written permission of the publisher, except as permitted by U.S. copyright law. For permission requests, contact kelly@authorkellycollins.com.

The story, all names, characters, and incidents portrayed in this production are fictitious. No identification with actual persons (living or deceased), places, buildings, and products is intended or should be inferred. All products or brand names are trademarks of their respective owners.

CHAPTER ONE

As a veterinarian, the routine job of giving vaccinations, trimming nails, and neutering pets could get tedious. I had to keep reminding myself that boring was good. Boring was *safe*. Boring was unlikely to get me killed.

I'd never been stabbed, shot, or shanked by my regular clientele. Domestic animals were generally safe, unlike my decidedly *non-animal* clients who often appeared at the end of my shift.

I hadn't had any of those today—yet—but there was still a good twenty minutes in which some bloody, bruised or otherwise damaged person might come in asking to be stitched or cleaned up 'under the radar'.

You know, for someone who tried her best to keep out of the mob life, I wasn't doing a great job. But I could hardly turn any of those men (and occasionally women) away. If they went to a hospital, they'd most likely get arrested or worse. I didn't want that on my conscience.

Despite my father, Liam "Lucky" O'Leary, heading up the Irish mob, I helped members of *any* of the mob factions in Las Vegas if they ventured into the Collins Veterinary Clinic, be they Irish, Russian or Italian. I often had people come in asking for help who weren't part of the factions. Recently, there had been an influx of Colombians trying to get a foothold in the Vegas underworld, so I'd gained more and more of them as 'patients'. I tended to a unique melting pot of saints and savages.

I wanted nobody's blood on my hands, so despite me not wishing to play any part in the mob life I was born and raised into, I became Las Vegas' unofficial mob doctor.

Even I could admit that it sounded pretty badass. That was precisely why I wished I could get out of it—the danger and excitement of it all could be addictive. But it was also a death sentence; all you had to do was get involved with the wrong people or be present on the wrong street at the wrong time, and you were done.

At least, for me, since I patched up anyone who came into the clinic, I had been granted 'immunity'—nobody wanted the woman who stitched up their men and prevented them from getting arrested to be harmed. And damn if that didn't feel good knowing I had that kind of sway within the Vegas mob network.

Ugh. Again, thoughts such as that were exactly *why* I had to get away. But I loved Las Vegas; it was my home. To move away and give it up would be tantamount to destroying a part of my soul.

With one final clip of the scissors, I finished trimming my last patient of the day's nails—a humongous rabbit named Hulk. Appropriately named considering he was almost half the size of his petite owner. They always made me laugh when they came in.

I gave the all black rabbit a fond scratch behind his floppy ears. "He's all done, May. Shall I book Hulk in for another nail trimming in three months' time?"

She nodded as she hefted her gentle giant into his crate—which was built for a small dog. "Thanks, Kirsten. That would be great. Hulk will be happy he can scamper about again—and my boyfriend will be happy his nails stop scratching up the wooden floor."

It was with a contented sigh that I collapsed onto the window seat in the exam room once May Waters had left. I watched the orange glow of the sun slowly set behind the buildings.

It was a long day, working two shifts back-to-back because the other junior vet, Rose, had gotten sick—the flu, apparently. I'm fairly certain she was lying; I vaguely recalled catching sight of her calendar on her phone a couple weeks ago and seeing her boyfriend was flying in to visit her over the next few days.

Not that I could blame her. If I had a boyfriend flying in to see me, I'd pretend to be sick, too. But that train of thought led nowhere good—all it did was make me think of Rafe. Raphael

Wilde, the youngest of the three infamous Las Vegas, Italian mob brothers, now working as an in-demand lawyer after graduating from Harvard. We'd known each other for…probably as long as I can remember. And we'd been forbidden from ever acting on our yearning stares and stolen glances for…probably as long as I can remember, too.

But Katya—my newly discovered half-sister—now belonged just as much to the Irish mob as the Russian mob she was born into. She married Matt, one of Rafe's older brothers, and had infiltrated the Italian mob as well. If she could be with one of the Wildes, then why couldn't I?

I sighed again, this time longingly. It would never happen. Rafe and I had been out of touch ever since I graduated as a vet. We did our best to avoid each other at Alex's wedding to Faye, and then again at Katya's wedding to Matt, knowing that seeing each other would end up being painful.

Had we not attempted to keep our distance, we'd have done something we'd regret. How I *wish* we could have done something we'd regret.

But it was common knowledge that Rafe wanted no part of his family's mob life, and he was doing one hell of a good job avoiding it. Unlike me. I wouldn't be surprised if he jumped on a flight out of Vegas and moved to New York any moment now, never to be seen or heard from again.

I had to forget about him, but I had been trying to forget about him ever since I was old enough to identify what the butterflies in my stomach meant when I saw him—and I'd failed, failed, failed.

Was I doomed to pine after a man I couldn't have, trying to find solace in short-lived boyfriends who simply couldn't match Rafe? It was that, or my mob family scared them off. With two intimidating brothers and a father who looked like he could gut a person without breaking a sweat, it was probably both, to be honest.

"Kirst, are you done in here?" Dean Collins, owner and senior vet of the clinic asked as he rapped on the door.

"You know I hate you calling me that, Dean," I replied, sighing a little as I moved from my window seat and walked to the door. "And yes, I'm done. Finally."

Dean grinned; his sandy blond hair, pale blue eyes, and flawless skin belied the fact that he was just a couple years shy of forty.

If I look as good as that when I'm thirty-eight, then I'll be one thrilled woman, I thought, returning Dean's grin with a tired smile.

"You sure you're done? No scary gangsters in to get their arm stitched up today?"

Now, here was a man who was unfazed about my mob background. If anything, he *liked* it. It meant his precious clinic was protected—and the fact that my non-animal clients brought in extra money. Or, at least, they paid for what they used.

I shook my head no. "Doesn't seem like there will be any today, thank Go—"

That's when the front doorbell rang, signaling a new customer. I stifled a groan.

"I can send them away if you don't feel up for it, Kirsten," Dean said, frowning slightly in concern as he placed a hand up to my forehead. "You look as if you need to sleep for about three days, and it feels like you might be coming down with a fever."

I gently brushed Dean's hand away as I made my way around him towards the reception. "It's better to deal with whoever it is now than risk what'll happen to them if I don't. And if I have a fever, you can blame Rose."

Maybe she was actually sick, I thought. *Sucks to be her if her boyfriend's visiting and she's chucking up in the toilet or shivering with a fever in bed.*

"Your funeral," I barely heard Dean comment as I reached the reception desk. The person standing there was indeed a member of the mob, but not the person I expected.

It was Katya.

She tucked a stray strand of hair behind her ear as she smiled at me awkwardly.

"Hey, Kirsten. I just found out you worked here, and..." she lifted her shoulders in a shrug. "I figured I'd stop by and say hi."

Out of the corner of my eye, I saw Dean watching the two of us curiously, so I ushered him over.

"Katya, this is my boss Dean. Dean, this is my...half-sister, Katya," I said, the words feeling odd on my tongue.

Dean shook Katya's hand as he smiled devilishly for her—the guy definitely knew how to wield his looks like a weapon.

A sharp deadly weapon that could excise the heart from any woman.

He turned up the charm a notch. "The illustrious half-sister. Lovely to meet more of Kirsten's family," he said, "especially a beautiful woman. I was worrying that all the people Kirsten was surrounded by were big, scary men."

Katya laughed. "Well, that comes with the territory, I'm afraid." She glanced at me. "Are you done for the day? I thought we could get a drink or something—get to know each other a bit more? I've never had a sister."

Neither had I, although I'd asked for one for Christmas one year. "Oh wow, yes, please," I replied, practically falling over myself at the thought of alcohol after a long, dull day in the clinic.

Dean laughed at the comment—even Katya let out a quiet giggle.

"I'll leave you ladies to your drinks," he said. "Don't worry about the cleanup, Kirsten—I'll get it done. And feel free to take the morning off since we don't have many appointments until noon."

"And what if I'm really sick?"

Dean sighed dramatically. "Ahh, with Rose off, then you'll just have to force the sickness away."

"Of course. I knew your concern was purely superficial."

He thumped his chest with his hand. "That breaks my heart."

I waved dismissively, rolling my eyes at the comment. "Have a good evening."

"You too."

With the summer on the edge of breaking, the early evening air was balmy, with only the barest hint of a chill on the edge of the breeze that blew by.

"Do you know any bars nearby?" Katya asked, happily linking arms with me when I offered her mine.

"I hope that was a rhetorical question," I scoffed. "I know them all…and not necessarily because they're good places to drink."

I knew most by reputation—and the number of injured brawlers they sent my way. One look at Katya confirmed that she got my meaning.

"Take me to one good for drinking but bad for fist fights… if there are any."

Oh, I definitely liked my new sister. I could tell we would get on like milk and cookies. One was better with the other.

I ended up taking her to Cole's—a bar with absolutely no mob ties whatsoever.

"I'll have a double vodka and orange," I told the bartender as soon as we reached the bar.

Katya laughed. "You weren't lying when you said you wanted alcohol." She looked at the bartender. "I'll have the same."

We ended up remaining seated at the bar as we talked—to stay close to the alcohol, I joked—but in reality, once we spoke, we lost track of time so much that we forgot to wrangle a booth.

"So, how's Matt? All good between you two?" I asked

Katya after my third drink, feeling decidedly more relaxed than I was earlier on.

Katya blushed. "Fantastic. You know, after being in love with each other for so long, but thinking there was no way we'd ever actually be together, it feels…I don't know. Surreal. Like I can't believe my luck."

Oh, that stung. I emptied my glass, thinking about Rafe. "I'm glad it could work out for one of us, Katya."

"Don't tell me you have a forbidden love for someone you can't have, too?" she asked, incredulous but somehow not surprised at all. She followed suit and downed her drink. "There must be something in the water. So who is it?"

"Who is what?"

"Who is the guy? Your boss?"

If I had had any of my drink left in my mouth, I'd have spat it out. "Dean? Oh God, no!"

"But he's so charming! And he definitely has a thing for you."

"He's like that with every woman he comes across. It's his bedside manner. Besides, the guy is twelve years older than me."

Katya's eyes widen. "No way is he nearly forty!"

"I know, right? The man's clearly a vampire. Or a wizard."

"Maybe he sold his soul to the devil for an evergreen youthful appearance."

I snorted in laughter. "I wouldn't be surprised. Either way, it isn't him."

"Then who is it?"

I paused, considering whether I should tell Katya. It may well have been that it was only a matter of time before she found out Rafe and I both had a thing for each other from Matt, but…I couldn't bring myself to talk about him. Not yet. Possibly never.

I sighed, looking at the time on my phone. Suddenly, I was exhausted. Thinking about Rafe often did that.

"Nobody important," I finally told her. "Well, not anymore. I should get going; I feel like I need about fourteen hours of sleep, and I don't want to spend my precious morning sleeping off a hangover."

She smiled at me. "Understandable. Do you…want to do this again?"

I perked up immediately. "Absolutely! Next time, let's do it when we both have a day off and can get utterly smashed."

"Deal."

As I walked back home to the apartment I lived in to stay independent from my father and brothers, I smiled to myself.

She might have been late in joining the family, but having a sister was awesome.

CHAPTER TWO

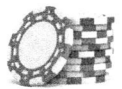

If this guy didn't shut up soon, I swore I was going to punch him in the mouth. How anybody could be that pigheaded as to brag about doing something he'd hired me to convince the court he didn't do was beyond me.

"For the last time, Mr. Peters, I don't want to know," I said, barely concealing my irritation. "It will impact your case if I know."

The guy laughed at me. "Okay, okay, Mr. Wilde, but man —if you had been there, I swear you would've—"

"Have a good day, Mr. Peters," I interrupted, standing up and making it obvious the meeting was over. "I'll see you on Monday for a follow-up."

God, Friday can't come quickly enough, I thought yearningly as the insufferable man vacated my office, still laughing about what he did. It was only Tuesday.

I did *not* sign up to defend the scum of the Earth. Okay, I'm a lawyer. I guess I signed up for it, in a sense. But I swore to myself I wouldn't deal with men like Mr. Peters. Instead, I'd defend innocent people *from* him.

Such a worldview was so naïve that even I didn't truly believe it, even as a kid. I grew up in the Italian *mob,* for Christ's sake. How was I ever going to grow up with a positive outlook with hardened criminals around me?

The answer is, I wasn't. And yet here I was, still wishing for just one innocent client. The thing was, innocent clients weren't the kind who could afford the firm I worked for, and, by extension, me. And there was only so much *pro bono* work McAlister and Associates took on—and that was left to the trainee lawyers. Again, me.

Which meant Raphael Wilde, aged twenty-eight, who despite only having joined the firm as a junior lawyer recently was on the fast-track to partner, and who subsequently didn't get the innocent clients. McAlister and Associates thought my skills were better used with people I was familiar with —mobsters.

Maybe all of this would be easier if I didn't have to deal with crooked clients in my home life, too. Not that I hadn't desperately tried to escape the mob life that constantly hounded me because of my pedigree as a Wilde. In actuality, I had been doing quite well at keeping out of it throughout my time at Harvard. So well, in fact, that I thought I had successfully broken away.

But the last year or so had demonstrated how easy it was for the dark underbelly of Las Vegas to sink its teeth into me.

I just never thought I'd be helping out the *Russian* mob. I mean, yeah, it was for Matt's sake I did it, and his now-wife Katya, but ultimately I was part of a massively fraudulent scheme…that put Sergei Volkov at the very top of the Russian mob. I didn't even want to know what really happened to Katya's father, Yuri, the previous head. Because if I knew the answer…

Then I knew I'd most definitely have been involved in more than simply the creation of fraudulent documents.

My head falls into my hands; I've had enough. I've had enough of this life I was born into for longer than I can remember. I'm not cut out for it—every time I've been asked to use my law degree for something 'not quite legal', I've felt as if my soul has slowly chipped away. There's only so much more I can take before there's nothing left.

Thinking back to when things were simpler, my mind invariably wandered to Kirsten O'Leary.

The kid I befriended before I truly understood why we couldn't be friends. The girl I fell in love with. The woman I cannot have.

Though Kirsten and I hadn't been 'allowed' to be friends, of course, we had still actually been friends. Her older brother Ian was one of my best friends, in reality, though a large part of that was the fact that we both went to college together. He was also one of the plethora of reasons why I couldn't act on my feelings for his sister.

He had made it abundantly clear I couldn't pursue Kirsten. It was madness to do so—our families were not on good terms. And, more personally, if I broke Kirsten's heart or had cause to make her cry, Ian would be sure I paid for it—probably with my life.

But ever since my older brother Matt married Katya—who we only found out very recently was half O'Leary—I had to admit, I'd been thinking about contacting Kirsten. Matt and Katya were acting as a bridge between our two families; a narrow, rickety bridge, but a bridge nonetheless. So why couldn't Kirsten and I act on our feelings?

I was running on the assumption that Kirsten still had feelings for me. We had spoken little over the past three years. I wasn't the only one trying to avoid the other at my brothers weddings…and why would she avoid me if she had no lingering desire for me?

"For shit's sake," I cursed aloud, hating myself for sullying the good memories of my childhood with Kirsten by tying it back to the present. Besides, getting together with the Irish mob boss' daughter would only drag me back into a life I did not want.

If I was going to get out, I needed to leave my feelings for Kirsten firmly in the past, where they belonged.

Ha. Easier said than done.

My thoughts were interrupted by a call.

"Yes, what is it?" I asked my assistant, who was on the other line.

"It's Ian O'Leary on the phone for you, Mr. Wilde. Should I patch him through?"

Of course, he'd call when I'm thinking about his sister, I thought. *Typical Ian.*

I sighed. "Yes, let his call through. Thanks, Alexa."

There were a few seconds of static before I heard the familiar voice of my best friend. "Wilde, what are you up to this evening?" Ian asked, foregoing a hello.

I checked the time on my watch. I had less than twenty minutes left at work before I could leave. "I was planning on getting ramen and a couple of beers for dinner, then heading home."

It was still weird to call the Wilde family compound my home after having spent much of my adult life trying to get away from the place. But with my parents now both dead, it was mine to keep, even though I hadn't wanted it. The damn place was like a luxury hotel. What did one man need with that much space?

Ian let out a noise of disgust. "What are you, sixty years old? Come join me for a drink."

"I can't be held to your beck and call for my whole life," I told Ian, suppressing another sigh. "This isn't college."

"Ha! As if I had to push you to do *anything* in college. And besides, I'm outside your office now."

Groaning, I spun around in my chair and walked to the window. Sure enough, there was Ian, grinning up at me and waving.

"If you're not down here in five minutes, I'm coming up to get you."

And with that, Ian hung up the phone. Resigned to my fate, even though I didn't imagine I had ever felt *less* like socializing than I did now, I turned off my computer, grabbed my suit jacket, and left my office, murmuring a goodbye to Alexa on my way out.

"You're a jackass, you know," I said to Ian as we made our way down the street towards a nondescript bar. Neither of us was picky about where we drank—just so long as the place served alcohol, it was fine by us. "You can't expect me to leave work early every time you want to drink."

Ian laughed easily. "Then stop accepting my invitations." He ordered us two beers, then we wandered over to a nearby table and sat down.

"So," I said, "any particular reason we're drinking tonight?"

"Nothing specific." He raised his glass to his lips and took a long, slow drink. "How are you feeling about the Matt and Katya thing?"

Leave to him to ask about that.

"I'm happy for them. It's going well. How are you feeling about having a half-sister?" I chuckled. "A half-Russian sister." Given the fact the Irish and Russians were always at each other's throats, this situation had to be uncomfortable for both families.

Ian stretched his arms up above his head. "I dunno, to be honest. She's a great girl and all that. And she's hot which makes it creepy that she's my sister. Kind of bummed she's my sister."

"Ian," I interrupted, giving him a warning glance.

"I know, I know. No being lewd towards women. Anyway, she was the Russian mob's little princess. Anyone would be crazy to go near her. Your brother was insane for having done so."

"He just wanted to be with the woman he loved. What's wrong with that?"

Ian gave me a level stare. "Don't."

"Don't what?"

"Don't even think about contacting Kirsten. Don't even consider it."

I held my hands up in mock surrender. "I didn't say a thing!"

"You were thinking it, you dick! And anyway, what happened to that girl you were seeing—Claire, was it?"

"Clara," I corrected, taking a swig of beer as I did so. "And she's long gone. It wasn't serious, anyway."

"You're never serious about anybody."

"Neither are you."

"Touché."

We sat in companionable silence for a while, our minds both clearly full of something we didn't want to discuss with each other.

Eventually, Ian said, "Please. Just forget about Kirsten. Things are frayed to shit just now as it is. And with everyone jockeying for position—"

"I don't wanna hear it, Ian. You know that. God, if there ever was a reason I wouldn't make a move on your sister, this is it. I'm tired of all this shit. I just…want out. And you know that."

Ian said nothing for a moment, then he smiled at me. "I know, I know. I'm sorry, man. You've gotta understand where I'm coming from, even if you don't want to know the specifics. Just—"

"Forget about her. I know. You've said that a few thousand times over the years."

"That sounds like a gross exaggeration."

"I wish it were. If I didn't know any better, I'd say you were the one with an obsession for your sister."

Ian wrinkled his nose in disgust. "Don't even say that. I'm not used to Katya being my sister. I can at least admire her beauty."

"Don't be a sick bastard," I teased.

"Dammit, you ruin everything."

"I'd say the fact that you share chromosomes ruins everything. And that she's my sister-in-law, too—if you get to be all super protective of Kirsten, then I get to be protective of Katya."

"Well argued, as usual. You'd almost think you were a lawyer."

"Very funny." I glanced at my watch—if I didn't get home soon, I'd likely crash out in this bar. It had been a long day. Ian noticed the movement.

"I get it, it's been a long day." He yawned. "I'm tired, too. Call it a night?"

"Sounds good. Are we still going to Capone's on Friday night?"

"Ah, yeah. I forgot. Thanks for reminding me. I'll see you there."

Ian ran off without another word, leaving me to gather my things and pay for the drinks before stepping out into the late-summer evening air.

He made it perfectly clear I should forget about Kirsten, Hell, even I made it perfectly clear why I should forget about Kirsten, but I couldn't. She was unforgettable.

There were so many reasons for me to move on. The odds were stacked against us from the beginning.

So why was it that, deep down, I couldn't let her go?

I sighed as I reached my family home.

Something told me I wasn't likely to fall asleep tonight for a long, long time.

CHAPTER THREE

There was something about not making it out of the vet clinic for lunch that usually made the day absolutely drag. But when we got a rare, quiet day, lazing about in the back room with Rose and Dean was actually fun.

It was Rose's first day back since she was off with the flu—and, seeing her, I realized she most definitely hadn't been lying about her illness. She had clearly lost a few pounds and still seemed a little fragile though Rose had at least had her boyfriend up visiting to look after her.

It transpired that I hadn't contracted Rose's horrendous flu after all. My symptoms had resulted from plain old exhaustion. Easily fixed with the alcohol I had consumed with Katya and fourteen hours of sleep. Yes. I had slept my entire morning off away.

Now it was finally Friday, and I was in a good mood—the kind the end of the week always brought about.

Rose sighed. Her boyfriend had traveled back to Los Angeles that morning. She clearly needed cheering up.

"When does your man move over to Las Vegas, Rose?" I asked her around my mouthful of cereal—I loved nothing more than eating breakfast cereal for lunch, despite how childish it was. I loved how the little marshmallow treats floated on top of the milk.

"Joshua's transfer has been delayed—at the rate it's going, he may not be able to get a transfer at all."

Oh…God. I only made things worse. "Have you considered moving to L.A. instead?"

She shook her head unhappily. "Joshua is set on moving here. And L.A. is expensive like you wouldn't believe—well, you probably *can* believe it. It's Los Angeles, after all. Sometimes I wish we could just buy a boat there and sail away, never to be bothered by soaring rent prices again."

"Ah," Dean interjected, waving his sandwich at Rose as he spoke, "but then you'd have to deal with the prices of marinas and ports when you needed to dock, which are pretty damn extortionate. And who would pay you to work? The dolphins? Though I don't doubt they'd appreciate you cutting them out of a fishing net or two—"

"We get it, Dean. You're hilarious. Way to ruin a fantasy."

"That's what I'm here for," he replied, shrugging his shoulders nonchalantly as he chuckled to himself. Dean was in a good mood. The clinic was closed in its entirety tomorrow for equipment maintenance checks. For once, all three of us had the day off from our jobs to look forward to.

I could confidently say that in the year since I graduated from vet school and joined the clinic, an all-inclusive day off had *never* happened.

I watched as Rose played with her salad unenthusiastically. I felt bad for her. She had been with Joshua for two years now and spent close to six months of their relationship in Las Vegas. I knew it was taking its toll on her, especially with long hours working and few friends in the city. When were you supposed to make friends if you were working constantly and using any free time you had with your long-distance boyfriend?

The answer was that you didn't. That was probably why Rose and I were so close—because she had no other friend options. Well, really, neither of us had other options, since the vast majority of the people I knew were either related to the mob which I wanted nothing to do with in my free time if I could help it, or were college friends who now worked elsewhere.

I suppose it helped that we did actually get on well with each other though Rose was far more serious and high-strung than I was. Suddenly, I was very glad that Katya and I seemed to have hit it off—clearly, I needed to expand my circle of influence.

"Earth to Kirsten!" Dean suddenly called out, waving a hand in front of my face as he laughed at me. I hadn't realized

I'd zoned out and was subsequently ignoring my cell phone buzzing impatiently on the table.

It was Katya, so I happily answered the call.

"Hey, Katya, what's up?"

"Hey, are you free tonight? I'm the new events planner for Capone's, and my very first organized event is tonight! It's a cabaret, but it's chill—you interested?"

"Hell yeah, I am! And I actually have tomorrow off, which is even better."

Katya let out an adorable noise of glee. "I'm so happy you can make it! Bring along anyone you want. Just say my name at the door, and you'll get in with no problems. Oh, and Matt's brothers will be there—he told me I should tell you that."

Of course, he did. But the thought made my stomach flutter despite me telling it not to.

"Even Rafe?" I asked, hating myself for checking. Out of the corner of my eye, I noticed both Rose and Dean perk up at the mention of someone I'd never told them about.

"Especially Rafe. Again, Matt's words. Why, do you guys have a thing going on?" Katya responded, suddenly excited at the prospect.

"Oh lord, no!" I spluttered, knowing the heat on my cheeks caused them to turn red in a ruddy flush. "What time should I get to Capone's, anyway?"

"Let's call it nine. I can't wait to see you."

"You too."

"See ya then."

I let out a breath. Katya was clearly not convinced of my

lie. Although…it wasn't a lie, not *really*. There was nothing going on between Rafe and me, and there never technically had been, which made me feel worse. Suddenly, my good mood slipped away from me.

"Who's Rafe, Kirsten?" Rose asked as she slowly stirred sugar into her coffee. The smirk on her face told me she wouldn't let it go. Her mood had markedly improved as fast as mine had soured.

"A…childhood friend," I replied, which wasn't a lie. "I haven't spoken to him in ages." Again, not an untruth.

"But you're totally crushing on him, right? You might have fooled your sister, but we got to witness the full-on face blush and everything. Right, Dean?"

"Uh huh," Dean said noncommittally. It seemed as if his mood had soured too. Maybe he didn't enjoy typical 'female gossiping' about men.

"Rose, honestly, I'm not crushing on him. Maybe I did when we were younger, but we've grown up since then."

Rose pouted. "And here I was thinking you finally showed interest in someone. You can be so boring sometimes, Kirst."

"I just haven't found the right guy yet. If that makes me uninteresting, then I'm okay with that."

"Ugh, God, that's so cliché. You need to get laid."

I stared at Rose, baffled, and then burst out laughing. Were we really talking sex in front of our boss?

"The two aren't mutually exclusive, funnily enough. I'm not above a hook-up now and then."

"You haven't had one since you worked here," Dean added.

I almost spat out my cereal in shock.

"How could you *possibly* know?"

He laughed. "Your reaction now confirms it. But I could just…tell. It's not as if you've had much free time, anyway. Given that I'm your boss, I'm well aware of how much time you spend in the clinic."

Damn Dean for being so perceptive. I hung my head in feigned shame. "I guess you got me there."

"Well, if all goes well, you can hook up with your childhood sweetheart tonight," Rose said, grinning. "You're going to Capone's, right? I wish I could get in there, but it's so difficult."

Suddenly, I had an idea—a way to prevent me from pining after Rafe all night—a way to keep me busy.

"Why don't you come with me? You, too, Dean," I suggested to the delight of Rose and the surprise of my boss. "We did always say we would have a staff night out at some point. I'd say it's long overdue."

"As if you had to ask me," Rose squealed, the color she had lost from her face after her flu rapidly returning. "What's the dress code? What's the theme of the night? When should we get there?"

Oh yeah. Rose hadn't gotten out in a while. Few friends and all.

I smiled at her. "Katya said to get there for the nine o'clock entertainment. We could meet for drinks beforehand.

Say eight? She said it was a cabaret but it would be pretty chill. Take from that what you will."

Rose got up and hugged me. "You do not understand how much I need a night out. This is gonna be great. And with me losing weight from puking my guts up, I have just the right dress."

"Too much info, you idiot. And stop calling me Kirst." I glanced at Dean. "She's picking up all your bad habits."

Dean chuckled. "I'm not taking responsibility for the impressionable Rose West."

"Are you going to join us? The clinic is closed tomorrow, and you have no one waiting for you at home, so you have no excuse."

"That was cold, O'Leary. Count me in. Hope you can hold your liquor."

"Oh please. I'm Irish. Isn't that all you need to know?"

"I'll believe that when I see you drink."

"Okay, okay, guys, stop with the competitiveness. You're making me lonely," Rose said, interrupting the typical path mine and Dean's conversations ended up taking.

"Sorry, Rose." I checked the time. "I have a cat in to see me in five minutes, so I'd best prep for that."

Dean glanced at the clock. "Is that Mrs. Daniels' tomcat? The ancient one?"

"That's the one. I don't know how he hasn't died yet—she's so old herself that she barely knows what she's feeding him half the time."

"Did you know he was a regular at this clinic before I took

it over from my uncle? He was just as mean-spirited back then as he is now."

That got a laugh out of both Rose and me.

"I guess someone has to be as old as you around here," I joked.

He feigned hurt. "I'm only twelve years older than you, Kirsten, and nine years older than you, Rose."

"Ugh, don't remind me that I'm nearly thirty! That was such a low blow. Age to women is like Kryptonite to Superman." I rose and stretched. "And on that note, I'm getting back to work."

The afternoon passed in a blur of excitement and nerves. I was genuinely happy to finally be going on a night out with Dean and Rose. I knew we'd have a great time together.

But then there was Rafe…

Always Rafe.

I didn't see how we could ignore each other at Capone's, not when it was Katya's first event. Her wedding had been an unexpected affair, and there had been so many people we could talk to that we easily avoided each other. That wouldn't be the case tonight.

What would happen if we found ourselves in close proximity, having both been consuming alcohol? I could only guess. And hope.

Despite myself, and my promises to get over him, all I needed was the mere suggestion of an opportunity for something to happen between us, and I was easily reminded those promises were empty.

So much for being an adult and moving on.

Surely with Rose and Dean by my side, nothing would happen. Nothing happening would be for the best. I knew how forward I could be when I was drunk. If I spoke to Rafe—or worse, danced with him—I knew I'd try to escalate the situation, but I couldn't. I just couldn't.

When I finally clocked out of work at six, all my worries and excitement had joined to form one huge, all-important question. What on Earth was I going to wear tonight?

CHAPTER FOUR

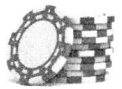

By the time I reached Capone's with Ian, the place was in full swing.

"Seems like my new baby sister can do her job well," Ian remarked appraisingly as we headed for the bar. He ordered us a bottle of red wine and two glasses—not what I had expected him to order at all.

I raised an eyebrow.

"What? This is a classy night. May as well pretend to be classy."

"Naturally." I knew darn well part of Ian was still keeping up appearances for Katya's sake, though I also knew it would only take a glass or two of wine before he showed his true, brash self to her. Something told me Katya could take care of herself, but I was content to allow Ian to play out his charade a little longer.

The wine he ordered was an excellent bottle. Smooth. Rich. Like velvet on the tongue.

On stage, a troupe of cabaret dancers began the opening act of the night. Daringly dressed in a plethora of sparkling, glittering outfits, they held the eyes of most everyone in the room.

They would have held mine, too, if Kirsten O'Leary hadn't just walked into Capone's and over to the bar with two strangers in tow. One stranger was a pretty woman probably around Kirsten's age. I thought I recognized her from photos on Kirsten's social media page, but the sandy-haired man laughing at something Kirsten had just said was completely unknown to me.

Shit, he was a good looking guy. Even worse, Kirsten clearly got on really well with him.

Did she have a boyfriend I didn't know about?

I turned to Ian, pointing out his sister at the bar.

"Did Kirsten get a boyfriend?"

Ian glowered at me. "What did I say yesterday?"

"It's just polite interest. She didn't have a plus one at the wedding."

My friend considered me for a moment, clearly thinking long and hard about whether to respond. Then he sighed. "In all honesty, I don't know. I think that's her boss, from the vet clinic. Surname is Collins. Kirsten hasn't mentioned seeing anyone when she's come home for dinner, so the two of them could have been together for years for all I know. Pretty sure that isn't the case though. However…"

Ian narrowed his eyes at this Collins guy. He had a hand on Kirsten's back as they made their way through the crowd to a table reserved for them. Katya jumped up excitedly to hug Kirsten when they reached her.

"It's kind of obvious he's into her," Ian finished, confirming my suspicions. "Which would be great since she's trying hard to stay out of the family business."

"Her too, huh?"

"She's not doing too great a job, though. She patches up anyone who comes into that vet clinic. I think half the mobsters in Vegas are in love with her because of it."

I glanced over at Kirsten, surprised. I didn't know she did that. Then again, what did I really know about her nowadays? We hadn't really spoken in years.

That guy fawned over her like she hung the moon and stars. And yet, Kirsten seemed oblivious. How could that be possible?

Abruptly, I stood up, much to the chagrin of Ian.

"Rafe," he warned.

"Ian, Katya is literally waving us over," I replied, waving back to her as I walked toward her. Ian rushed out of his seat to follow me.

"I'm watching you, you know," he grumbled.

I rolled my eyes. "Yeah, yeah, I know."

"Well, if it isn't two of my four new brothers," Katya said happily as she hugged us both. "I'm glad you could make it."

"Where's Matt?" I looked around the dimly lit venue. "And Alex?"

She pointed over her shoulder with a thumb. "Over there somewhere drinking shots. Why, you gonna abandon me for them?"

"Of course not," Ian cut in, smiling charmingly for her.

God, he needed to get over his crush, pronto. Though it was hardly as if I could blame him—Katya was beautiful. But she wasn't the only one. With the nightclub's lights dancing around us, Kirsten's red-brown hair looked on fire. Her beautiful green eyes were locked on me.

With a small smile curling her lips, she said, "Well, if it isn't Rafe Wilde. Long time, no speak." Clearly, she intended to act as if we hadn't been deliberately ignoring each other for the past few years, which was fine by me. More than fine.

"It's great to see you, Kirsten," I replied, pulling her in for a hug. Oh God, she smelled amazing, and the figure-hugging dark green dress she wore meant I could see and feel every curve of her body.

Get your mind out of the gutter, I thought ashamedly as she and I pulled away from each other. *Get it together.*

"So this is the mysterious Rafe from your phone call, Kirsten," came a male voice. It was the man who had entered Capone's with her. She glanced at him and smiled.

"I guess it is. Rafe, this is Dean Collins, my boss, and this..." she gestured to the woman standing next to her, "is Rose West, the other junior vet at the clinic." Her eyes fell back to mine. "Guys, this is Rafe Wilde."

Dean's eyes widened in recognition. "One of *the* Wilde

brothers? I've had plenty of your men in my clinic depending on Kirsten to patch them up, but I've never seen you before."

I hated that he was so familiar with our world—with Kirsten and her world. It also irritated me that he was so accepting.

"I'm out of the family business."

Kirsten's friend Rose grinned at me, though I didn't know why. Then she looked at Kirsten. "You failed to mention how *hot* your childhood friend was, Kirst," she said, much to the obvious horror of Kirsten.

So I was a 'childhood friend'. That stung like a bitch even though I knew the statement to be true. I'd always wanted more. Still wanted more.

Kirsten looked embarrassed. "Shut up, Rose."

"Never."

"Won't you join us, Mr. Wilde?" Dean asked, a tone of superiority to his voice that very much implied Kirsten was with him and not me. I suppose I had no right to be jealous, but that didn't change that I was.

"I don't suppose I can borrow Kirsten for a few minutes?" I asked, ignoring the outraged look Ian suddenly threw at me. I'd pay for this later, but for now, he wouldn't risk embarrassing Kirsten or Katya for that matter.

"You can definitely borrow me, Rafe." Kirsten grinned, and then, upon noticing her brother's expression, she added on, "Don't even start, Ian. Rafe and I are due a catch-up—you know we haven't spoken in years. Go get Katya a drink. She prefers top-shelf vodka."

I laughed at Kirsten's no-nonsense approach to dealing with her possessive older brother; I'd forgotten how little crap she took from anyone. Out of the corner of my eye, as the two of us walked away, I noticed Dean and Rose watching me. Dean looked somewhat annoyed, but Rose looked excited.

Surely, if Kirsten and Dean were an item, then Rose would have been privy to that information. She wouldn't look as if she desperately wanted something to happen between us.

Going after what I wanted would be a bad thing. With the wine I had already drunk hitting my brain, I was feeling risky and careless. *Yep, definitely a bad thing.*

The two of us stopped in a corner of Capone's somewhat away from the bustle of the crowd and stage. Kirsten looked up at me through her long, thick eyelashes for a moment, then glanced away.

"It really has been a while, Rafe," she mumbled.

"You're telling me. Congrats on graduating and getting such a good job. I should have said that months ago."

"It's okay. Congrats to you, too. Only just graduated yourself, and you're already on the fast-track to partner at your new job, I hear. You must be damn good."

"Ha, you flatter me."

"Is it flattery if it's true?" Kirsten looked back up at me again. God, she was beautiful. Her off-the-shoulder dress had me looking at her bare skin whether or not I wanted to. I felt an age-old heat build inside me. Gut twisting. Sweating palms. Embarrassing hard-on attraction.

"You look...so damn great, Kirsten," I admitted. Kirsten

looked a little taken aback, but then she blushed and laughed quietly.

"You're looking great yourself, Mr. Wilde."

I stood taller and more proud that she still found me attractive. "Clearly, the years of law school stress have been good to me."

It was ridiculous how easy it was to fall back into the easy banter of our past. Our conversation continued in this manner for several minutes as we happily caught each other up on our lives. When Kirsten suggested we head to the bar to top off our drinks, I didn't refuse.

Everything I was doing was wrong. I shouldn't have asked to speak to Kirsten privately. A quick glance over at the table where Ian sat glaring at me was all I needed to confirm that. Kirsten's boss watched her with a somewhat pained expression on his face.

"So what's the deal between you and your boss?" I asked as she passed me a shot of tequila.

"What do you mean, what's our deal? He's my boss."

Oh, poor guy. Kirsten really had no idea.

"He seems pretty into you," I said, not knowing why I was pushing the subject.

"Don't mind Dean. He's flirty with every woman he sees. I'm not sure if he's ever been serious about anyone."

Looking back at the table, I saw that Dean was now laughing along with Katya. I wondered if I'd imagined things, twisting an easygoing man's intentions into something more than they were because of jealousy.

I really needed to get over Kirsten. This kind of thinking wasn't good for me. But all I had to do was look at her as we chimed our shots together, and I knew I would not be able to ignore her for long. At least not tonight.

"To catching up," Kirsten announced.

"To catching up," I repeated.

We tossed our shots of tequila down our throats. I couldn't help letting out a bark of laughter when I saw Kirsten wince and worm in distaste.

"You know, for an Irish girl, you sure can't handle your booze."

"I can handle it fine, thank you. I simply don't like tequila."

"Why order it, then?"

"Because I know you do."

"How magnanimous of you."

Kirsten's eyes wandered towards the dance floor. The new act on stage was performing a dance to an upbeat rhythm. I found my foot tapping along to the beat despite myself.

"Wanna dance, Rafe?" Kirsten asked, emboldened by the tequila. "For...old times sake."

How could I say no to that?

"It would be my pleasure," I replied, allowing Kirsten to take my hand and lead me to the dance floor. Just as we were about to reach it, there was a loud banging noise. We turned our heads in the direction of the ruckus.

In rushed what seemed to be an entire precinct of police officers. It wasn't unusual for the police to show up. This was

Capone's, after all. A club owned by the Wildes—a mob family the police had never been able to take down. Their eyes scanned the area until most of them fell on us. On Kirsten specifically.

Instinctively, I pushed her behind me as three policemen wandered over to us, the entire club going silent as they watched. In the distance, I saw Ian, Katya, Dean, and Rose stand up and make their way toward us.

"Kirsten O'Leary, you're under arrest for the illegal distribution of narcotics," the first policeman said.

I turned to look at Kirsten as she stared at me in horror. I could barely hear the police recite her Miranda rights.

"What the hell is this about, Kirsten?"

"I don't—I don't know, Rafe." Hysteria distorted her voice. "I have no clue what's going on."

The policemen forced me to stand aside as they put Kirsten in handcuffs and walked her out of Capone's. Katya, Ian and Kirsten's work colleagues shouted after them, but their yelling fell on deaf ears.

I was numb.

I so easily fell back into step with Kirsten although I'd promised I wouldn't. She was clearly still a part of the dark underbelly of Las Vegas. The exact place I wanted to escape from. How could I have been so stupid?

As I watched through the open door as the policeman pushed Kirsten into the back of his car, I had a more pressing question. *How could she?*

CHAPTER FIVE

My mind was numb.

What the hell just happened?

How did I find myself in the back of a police car, hands bound in cold, steel cuffs and a drug charge filed against me?

It was madness.

The only thing even close to illegal I'd done in my entire life was helping out the people who came into the clinic to get patched up—but not once had I used any of the drugs I'd supposedly distributed while helping them out.

Okay, there was also the underage drinking before I turned twenty-one, but nearly everybody was guilty of that.

This reeked of a set-up. The only thing was...I had no idea who could be responsible. I had no enemies, and with the mob factions getting muddied by marriage and secret children, there wasn't a big likelihood it was them. We'd all become melded as family almost overnight. The one constant in all crime families was, family was first.

It was in a haze of panic and confusion that I arrived at the police station where they took my belongings and placed me in a holding cell. It was empty; I was the only person in it. Somehow, that made me feel worse. I shivered from the cold, not sure if it was caused by the emptiness I felt inside or the hard slab of concrete I sat on.

I thought of Rafe and the way he looked at me as I was being arrested. He believed the charges. He had to know I wasn't an out-and-out drug dealer, but he believed there was at least some truth to what I was arrested for. He looked at me as if he had wished he'd never chosen to speak to me tonight. He looked as if he wanted nothing to do with me again.

It wasn't fair. I wasn't guilty. I wanted out of the mob life just as much as Rafe did. How dare he assume I'd fall into illegal activities? Although we hadn't spoken in a few years, he had to know I wasn't the kind of person who would allow highly dangerous narcotics to be distributed around Las Vegas.

I mean, come on. I vaccinated bunnies and helped with the delivery of puppies and kittens, for God's sake. I stitched up people somewhere they felt safe.

All I wanted—all I ever wanted—was to help people. I'm the last person who'd want to damage the Vegas population. I knew how lethal some drugs I worked with could be on people. If those drugs had really found their way onto the streets…

I shuddered. It wasn't something I wanted to think about.

Besides, surely Dean would have mentioned if our stocks were unexpectedly low of the usual drugs and tranquilizers we used. Given the nature of the chemicals, Dean kept a very strict record of what was and wasn't used. It just didn't add up.

I was broken out of my reverie by the appearance of a policeman who ushered me out of the holding cell and into an interrogation room. A grim-looking man with thinning brown hair sat at a table in the middle of the room. He tapped a pen on an empty pad of paper.

When the policeman left, I turned my gaze over to the man sitting opposite me.

"What *the hell* is going on?"

He looked at me with a blank, measured expression on his face. "I hoped you'd be able to answer that exact question, Dr. O'Leary. I'm Detective Charles Peters. I'll be taking charge of your case."

"There is no case!" Agitation rose from my belly to my throat, the acid burning with every breath I took. "I have no idea what I'm doing here."

"Dr. O'Leary, I need you to calm down."

"Oh, I'm so sorry. Maybe I'm a little upset that I got publicly dragged away from my friends and family by the police for a crime I didn't commit."

The detective sighed and then placed a piece of paper in front of me. "These are the charges against you. We have several eyewitnesses who saw you selling the listed drugs to known dealers."

I glared at the man, then looked down at the paper and frowned. A few names caught my attention immediately.

Ketamine.

Morphine.

Fentanyl.

Oh no. Not Fentanyl. That stuff was tens of times stronger than heroin. I felt the blood drain from my face and grow cold as I scanned the rest of the list.

"How do you know these drugs are on the streets?" I asked Peters. My voice was barely audible. I knew I was shaking, but I couldn't help it. I was out of my element.

"We've arrested several individuals caught using the substances. And—" he paused for a moment, "—only three hours ago, we had one Fentanyl-related death happen ten minutes from Collins Vet Clinic."

Jesus Christ. Someone was already dead. I stared up at Peters.

I shook my head. "I'm not responsible for this. We aren't even missing any of these drugs from the clinic," I said, taking the risk that there were indeed no drugs missing.

"I'll be the one to see about that, Dr. O'Leary. I need not remind you of how dangerous these medications are. If you cooperate with us to get the dealers who are selling them off the streets, then we can arrange a lighter sentence for you."

"Lighter sentence?" My voice rose to a hysterical level. "I didn't do it."

"Dr. O'Lea—"

"Don't 'Doctor O'Leary' me! *I didn't do it.* Your eyewitnesses are lying. Someone is setting me up."

He set down the pen. "If that's the case," Peters replied, taking off his glasses to wipe them clean before returning them to the bridge of his nose, "then who might want to see you in prison? It's a very serious, very elaborate set-up if it is one."

I wanted to scream. Hell, I had screamed, but it served no purpose. Right now, I needed to keep a level head about me.

"If I had any idea, I would have led with that. I want my lawyer."

"Dr. O'Leary, are you sure we can't keep—"

"I. Want. My. Lawyer," I hissed through gritted teeth. I could feel a migraine coming on as the alcohol I'd consumed rapidly wore off.

There was a pause, then Peters said, "Very well. I'll have my colleague escort you back to the holding cell. Someone will be along shortly to get the details of your lawyer and give you the opportunity to make a phone call."

The same policeman as before took me back to the cell where I sat on a slab of cold cement and stared up at the blank ceiling.

Someone had died taking drugs I supposedly was responsible for getting out onto the streets. More would undoubtedly follow. This was serious.

If it was a set-up...who could I trust as my lawyer? My father's attorney was excellent, but if this was an inside job—no matter how unlikely that may be—then that wasn't a wise move.

If I went to another firm, the chances increased that the lawyers there would be paid off. If someone was going to this much trouble to frame me, I wouldn't put it past them to go that far.

Which only left…

Rafe.

But he wanted nothing to do with shit that might be connected to the mob. I saw the way he looked at me. We already tried to avoid each other despite the immediate sparks that flew tonight when we reconnected. He would never accept my case, but he was the only one I could trust.

Several hours passed before I could make a phone call. I wondered whether they hoped the solitude would make me more inclined to speak to the detective without a lawyer. Well, if that's what they were hoping for, then they were sadly mistaken.

I whiled away the time trying to doze on the hard surface, but I couldn't. My brain kept mulling over what everyone would think of my arrest.

What would Dean think? Would he have rushed straight to the clinic from Capone's to triple-check stock numbers, believing me to be guilty? I didn't think I could cope with my boss thinking for even a second that I was an untrustworthy criminal. I wouldn't be able to deal with losing his respect.

Just as much as I couldn't deal with having lost Rafe's.

When I could finally make a phone call, I considered calling Katya or my eldest brother Patrick, but I settled on Ian instead. Not only were we close, he was Rafe's best friend. If anybody could convince Rafe to believe me and defend me against these ridiculous drug charges, it was him.

The phone rang just twice before my brother picked up.

"Kirsten, this better be you," Ian said before I could say a word.

"Who else would you be expecting to hear from on the other end of a police line?" I joked. And then, "Yeah, it's me."

"What took you so long to call?"

"They only just let me, that's why."

"Have they questioned you? What's going on?"

"They questioned me until I said I needed my lawyer. Ian...some really nasty drugs are out there on the streets. Someone's died, and the detective said they have eyewitnesses who saw me handing the drugs over to several known drug dealers."

"Sounds like a damn set-up if you ask me."

I could almost cry.

"Thank you. I was feeling paranoid that everyone was gonna think I actually did it...Rafe certainly seemed to think I had."

Ian bit out a noise of outrage. "Of course he doesn't think you've done this. I think he was just shocked—and it was a stark reminder of everything he was trying to get away from."

"Just because of who our dad is? He'll deal with worse cases than mine in his law career. Why should it matter so much to him that this *may* or *may not* be related to the mob?"

Ian sighed. "You need him as your lawyer, don't you?"

"Ian, I can't trust anyone else. If this is mob related, then…"

"I know, I know. Consider him defending you. I'll speak to him. Give the detective his details, and I'll knock some sense into the bastard."

"Thanks, brother. This almost makes up for you constantly scaring Rafe off from having a relationship with me." I couldn't help the remark.

Ian let out a bark of laughter. It didn't hide the fact that he sounded exhausted. It suddenly occurred to me I had no idea what time it was.

"You know I'm only ever looking out for your best interests. With relations between the families like this—and if this drug crap is a move to make relations even more fraught, then—"

"Yeah, yeah, I get it," I interrupted. "Romeo and Juliet and all that. For everyone's sake, we can't be together. I remember."

"You didn't seem to remember earlier on. The Irish don't like it that we've pulled in a Russian. The Russians are even less thrilled that Katya is now Irish. Things are tense."

"Ian, are you really going to lecture me right now? I had been drinking, and Rafe and I hadn't spoken in years. We're only human. Besides, we're all family."

"Spoken from a girl who believed unicorns were possible." There was a pause, and then Ian made a noise of apology. "You're right, Kirsten. I'm sorry. I'll speak to him and get your bail sorted. You won't be detained for any longer than you have to be."

"Thanks, Ian. I love you."

"Love you, too, little sis."

With that, I hung the phone up and gave the policeman Rafe's contact details as my attorney once we got back to the holding cell. And then there was silence.

I was really going to have to spend a night in a prison cell.

How could it have been that mere hours ago I was worrying over what dress to wear? Now my carefully chosen off-shoulder green dress seemed entirely inappropriate for the chilly, hard-edged police cell.

For the first time in a long time, I wished my mother wasn't dead. I needed her to embrace me and tell me everything would be okay. But I had no one like that here. I was alone.

Shivering slightly and struggling to hold back tears, I lay down on the hard concrete and pulled my knees to my chest and prayed morning would arrive quickly. I prayed Ian could convince Rafe to defend me. Otherwise, I was utterly and royally screwed.

CHAPTER SIX

Oh no. Absolutely not.
　　I said I was done with the mob life.

I couldn't get involved again, even for Kirsten.

So why was I anxiously waiting up for a call from someone—*anyone*—just so I could know what the hell was going on? To see if there was anything I could do to help?

I regretted the way I had looked at and thought of Kirsten as she was arrested and taken away. Who was I to say she was guilty? If anything, I was one of the few people who could categorically say she wasn't. Despite our years apart, I knew Kirsten was still a good person. Certainly better than me.

After all, of the two of us, who had only just forged documents to cover up the probable murder of Katya's 'father', Yuri Petrenko? That would be me. Not Kirsten.

Capone's had been a mess after she was hauled away. Ian

had furiously called his elder brother and father to sort things out. Katya worried about trying to calm down the audience and continue the cabaret before it turned into more of a failure than it already had. Kirsten's friend Rose had cried...

Dean had looked concerned and confused. Did he know something? Was he responsible for what happened?

I shook my head. It wasn't my problem to deal with. Liam O'Leary would ensure his daughter would receive only the best legal counsel. They'd sort out the case against her in a heartbeat. I didn't have to worry about Kirsten at all.

That didn't change the fact that I was worrying about her.

We had fallen back into step so easily at Capone's. Had we actually ended up dancing together, I knew with reasonable certainty the two of us would have ended up back at Kirsten's apartment or back at the Wilde mansion. Ian and the rest of the O'Learys be damned.

And yet it was as if fate had decreed that the two of us couldn't even give in to our most base desires towards one another. We weren't even allowed to be a one-night stand.

Thanks, universe.

I was jerked out of my own head by the sound of my cell phone ringing. I glanced at the clock on the wall of my kitchen. It was close to two in the morning. I knew it could only be one person.

Ian.

With a deep sense of foreboding, I picked up the call. "I was expecting to have heard from you earlier than this," I said.

"I only just got off the phone with Kirsten myself."

I wasn't surprised Kirsten had used her one phone call to talk to him. They were closer than even I was to my own brothers.

Ian continued. "You know what I'm going to say, Rafe."

"I won't defend her, Ian. I can't. I thought you of all people would agree with me on this."

"Oh, trust me, after the way the two of you were behaving earlier, I wish I had the privilege of having Kirsten go to another attorney. But I don't."

"Why does it have to be me?"

There was a long pause.

"It's bad, Rafe. Really terrible. They have eyewitnesses who will attest to Kirsten selling all these stupidly dangerous drugs to known dealers. Someone died taking them."

"Shit."

"If all that happened was a case of mistaken identity, then any lawyer would do," Ian said, "but it's not. This is a set-up. And if Kirsten is being set up, then we can't rule out it could be an inside job. Someone—"

"Someone might not like that all of our families have reached an uneasy peace and want to break it," I interrupted. "I get it. But this is exactly why—"

"Screw you wanting to get out of all this shit!" Ian yelled, interrupting me this time. "You don't get it, Rafe. You don't get it at all. If it's an inside job, then Kirsten can't trust anyone to defend her but you. You're the only lawyer in this city—hell, maybe even out of the city—who couldn't possibly be bribed or blackmailed to mess up her defense. She needs you. We all do."

Ian was right. I had known it all along.

I sighed. "You must have known I would end up taking the job anyway. You know I wouldn't be able to live with myself if Kirsten went to prison for something she didn't do."

"You wouldn't even let her go to prison for something she did do, idiot." He laughed a little. It made me smile despite the seriousness of the situation. "Besides, it's not as if you need to do anything illegal or unethical. All you need to do is your job. Do it well. Your firm will be ecstatic that you've received such a high-paying, high-profile client."

"Yeah, just as long as I don't screw up."

"If you screw up, then trust me, your job security will be the *last* thing you'll be worrying about."

While Ian was a friend, he'd not blink an eye to hold me accountable if I screwed this up.

"I get it, so cool it with the threats." I looked back at my clock, considering how late it already was. I knew I would not get much sleep tonight. "I need to prepare some shit if we're going to get Kirsten out of the precinct tomorrow. They have probable cause, so they'll fight tooth-and-nail to keep her detained, but I think I can pull some strings."

"You're a lifesaver, Rafe."

"Flipping from thinly veiled death threats to unending praise?" I remarked, feigning shock. "Now there's the Ian I know and barely tolerate."

"Shut the hell up."

"You'll have her bail ready for tomorrow morning, I assume? It's not gonna be cheap."

"Dad and Patrick have already sorted it out. Patrick will get it from the bank tomorrow as soon as they're open."

"Great. Okay, I really need to go now, Ian. I have my work cut out for me if we're gonna get your sister out tomorrow."

"Honestly," Ian began, "thank you, Rafe. I know this can't be easy on you. But there's nothing else we can do."

"I know. Night, Ian."

"Night, Rafe."

With that, I was left with silence in the big kitchen—for precisely thirty seconds, when a sudden clamor in the hallway alerted me to the fact that somebody had decided that two in the morning was an acceptable time to wake me up had I been asleep.

I didn't even make it to the kitchen door before Matt and Katya let themselves in and barged into the kitchen, their faces full of concern and exhaustion.

"What the hell are you two doing here?" I asked. "I thought you'd have headed back to your apartment."

"As if I could leave you alone after everything that went down, Rafe," Matt said as Katya sat down, letting out a long sigh. "We'd have gotten here earlier, only it's not exactly like we could close Capone's early."

"You should have gone straight to bed, Matt. Katya looks like she's about to pass out."

Her eyes widened at the comment as she shook her head wildly from side to side. "There's no way I could sleep after what just happened. Have you heard from Kirsten? Any clue who set her up? She must feel awful in that damn police station."

Suddenly, I felt ashamed. Katya had known Kirsten for all of two seconds, and she never questioned Kirsten's innocence. While I—who had known her all her life—had still doubted her for a moment. I felt despicable.

"I haven't heard from her directly," I replied, "but I just got off the phone with Ian. I will be defending her."

Katya clapped her hands together in relief as Matt headed over to the kitchen liquor cabinet and returned with a bottle of vodka.

"I knew we had nothing to worry about." Matt grinned as he poured us all shots. I chucked it down my throat like a man dying of thirst. "I know it's not gonna be easy for you, working closely with her, Rafe. But you're doing the right thing."

"Okay, someone around here needs to give me the lowdown on this whole Rafe and Kirsten thing before I just make something up," Katya cut in.

I sighed. "Matt can tell you when you go to bed. I don't think I can handle hearing the story again. It's all I've been able to think about for days now."

Matt clucked his tongue sympathetically. "Things are different now. If you clear Kirsten's name, there's nobody who would stand in your way as a couple. Not even Ian."

"Ha. What a thing to say."

"You look like you need sleep even more than Katya does."

"Possibly, but I have a ton of paperwork to create before I can consider calling it a night." I stood up, stretching my arms above my head as I worked a crack out of my neck. "I'll be in Dad's old study. Take whatever room you want." I walked a few steps before I added, "Don't you two crazy kids stay up too late."

"Yes, Mom," Matt and Katya responded in unison, eliciting a laugh from all three of us.

"Night, guys."

"Night," they returned.

I wandered down the hallway towards the ground floor study with a heavy heart. The plush carpet absorbed the sounds of my heavy footfalls to leave me once again in silence.

I had my work cut out for me.

I wish Kirsten were here. She'd know what to do in a second—she had always been sharp and quick-witted like that. It wasn't as if her solutions were always flawless; indeed, sometimes they had actually gotten us into more trouble as kids, but she always did something, and that mattered.

I owed it to her to do something in return.

I would clear her name. I would find out who the asshole was who thought it was clever to frame the love of my life who ultimately could never be mine. And I would make them pay.

CHAPTER SEVEN

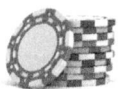

I always thought the sweetest words I would ever hear would be something like 'I love you' or 'You mean the world to me'. Alas, we don't get to choose these things.

"Your bail has been paid, Dr. O'Leary."

There. Those words right there were the sweetest words I'd ever heard in my life. I had experienced probably the roughest night of my life—and also the most sleep deprived. I was desperate to get out of my dress and scrub the smell of prison from my skin in a steaming hot shower. I'd probably eat a burger and fries and then crash for two days.

I knew I'd never get to live out today like that. Some food and a shower weren't too much to ask for, so I'd settle for those before tackling the mess my life had become.

When I saw my brothers, Patrick and Ian, waiting for me in the lobby, I almost cried. Almost. Ultimately, I was an

O'Leary and still had my pride; besides, I had cried enough for a lifetime when I was alone in that shockingly cold holding cell.

I wasn't above throwing myself at my brothers to receive a crushing, sibling bear hug.

"What's up, criminal?" Ian murmured into my hair, causing me to laugh in relief.

"You can take care of yourself, huh Kirsten?" Patrick mocked as we broke out of the group hug. "That's the last time I believe a word my little sister says."

I cuffed his upper arm. "Low blow, Patrick. You know this was a set-up."

"Obviously."

"Kirsten, you're ice cold," Ian said as he touched my forehead, frowning.

"Yeah, well, that holding cell wasn't exactly the most comfortable of places, you know."

"They didn't mistreat you, did they?"

"I suppose apathetic neglect counts as mistreatment. But honestly," I added quickly when it looked like both of my brothers would risk arrest themselves to kick up a fuss, "all I want to do is get the hell out of here. I suppose it's too early for a burger…"

I glanced up at the clock in the police station lobby. It was just after nine in the morning.

"Considering we've all been up all night, I'd say now is the perfect time for a burger," Patrick said, eliciting chuckles from both Ian and myself.

My eldest brother drove us to the nearest greasy burger place. Ian wrapped me up in his jacket when I couldn't stop shivering in the car. It might have been late summer, but after spending my night in that holding cell in my tiny dress with the air conditioning blasting, it certainly didn't feel like summer in Las Vegas.

Patrick ordered our food in the drive-thru, letting us eat to our hearts' content in his car. This was unusual behavior for my typically uptight, cleanliness-obsessed accountant of a brother, but this *was* an unusual situation.

I couldn't say I'd ever drunk soda for breakfast before, but I savored every bubble on my tongue as I soaked up the morning sun.

"Freedom feels wonderful." I sighed happily after I'd eaten enough for someone twice my size.

"Freedom with limitations, little sister," Patrick remarked, instantly souring my mood.

"Of course," I muttered, "but how limited?"

"You can't leave the city."

"I worked that one out for myself."

"You can't be out of your apartment or the O'Leary family home after ten in the evening unless you're with your attorney or a police officer."

"Ugh…great. Anything else?"

Patrick grimaced as if he really, really didn't want to tell me what came next.

"What is it?"

"You're not allowed to work," Ian eventually said. "You're on unpaid leave indefinitely until the case is cleared up."

"What?" This couldn't be happening. My job was my life. I loved it. If I couldn't work, then I'd probably go insane.

"Your boss didn't want this, but the detective working your case demanded it. Given what's happened, it's…understandable."

Understandable. Huh. I suppose it was if I thought about it rationally. But this was my life we were talking about. Rational didn't quite cover it.

And yet there was nothing else I could do about it. Sighing, I said, "Just take me home, please. I'd kill for a shower."

"Don't let the detective hear you say that," Patrick mused, clearly thinking he was hilarious.

"Oh yeah," Ian blurted. "Rafe's gonna defend you, like I said he would. He's the reason we got you out on bail so quickly, so you should probably call him to say thank you."

"A thank you can wait until I'm clean and out of this stupid dress."

Ian raised his eyebrows.

I scowled.

"You know I don't mean it like that, idiot brother."

"I know, I know. You and your cleanliness. To think you constantly make fun of Patrick for the same thing."

"That's not fair," Patrick said.

I waved the comment off. "There's a marked difference between wanting a shower after spending the night in a police station and vacuuming my car three times a week. And on that note," I said, sticking my tongue out when Patrick made a face of mock-outrage at my comment, "that's my apartment. I'll call you both later. Thank you so much for picking me up."

"Any time, little sister," Ian said as I opened the door and left Patrick's car.

"Just do your best to make this the only time," Patrick added with a smirk.

"You're so funny. Bye, guys."

"Bye."

It was all I could do not to run up the stairs and fling myself into the shower the second I got through the door. Instead, I forced myself to put my clothes into the laundry basket, painstakingly removed my ruined make-up, combed through my hair and brushed my teeth. Only then did I allow myself to enter my roomy steam-shower, which in reality was probably big enough for three people.

I reveled in the heat of the water and scent of the coconut shampoo I lathered into my hair. It was bliss.

And it was cut all-too-short. I had barely washed out my conditioner when the buzzer to my apartment rang, startling the life out of me. I was tempted to ignore it, but whoever was at my door merely pressed on the buzzer again, this time more insistently.

Sighing, I turned off the water and wrapped a towel around me, preparing my best 'I'm not in the mood for this' face as I did so.

"If this is a damn insurance salesman again, then I swear to God—" I began as I opened the door, but my sentence got stuck in my throat.

It was Rafe.

It was just my luck he'd show up when I was dripping wet from the shower, soapy suds still clung to my skin—of which there was *a lot* on show. I sincerely regretted not spending an extra ten seconds looking for a bigger towel.

Rafe's eyes traveled my body. While I'd been freezing earlier, his look created a sizzling heat that landed between my thighs.

He moved his eyes from my towel to my face. "Shit, sorry, Kirsten, I didn't mean to catch you right out of the shower," Rafe exclaimed, turning to leave.

"Technically, you didn't since I was still *in* the shower when you buzzed," I replied, smirking despite myself. "Come in, Rafe. We have a lot to talk about."

I didn't think I'd ever felt as awkward in my life as I did in the following moments, making coffee for the two of us in silence before handling Rafe a mug of the stuff. He remained standing as I sat down on my sofa.

"You can sit down, you know," I said, attempting to smile even though I was exhausted. Rafe looked me up and down before he could avert his gaze.

"Are you going to put clothes on?"

"Absolutely not. I'm getting straight back into that shower as soon as you're gone, Rafe. Unless you care to join me?"

"Kirsten…"

"I know," I sighed. "No jokes. This is serious and all that."

"It's not fair on either of us to be making suggestive comments like that right now."

"Oh, so what was last night? Just a blip in your self-control? I'm so sorry I caused you to undergo a moment of weakness." I hated the snarky response that flew from my mouth, but dammit, that moment with him was the best part of my day.

"Kirste—"

"Don't 'Kirsten' me, you dick," I fired out defensively. "I'm exhausted. I just spent the night in a freezing police cell for a crime I didn't commit—a crime that, even if it was only for a moment, you believed me to be guilty of, barely sixty seconds after you happily engaged in verbal foreplay with me. So don't you dare take the moral high ground here."

Ah, that seemed to work. Rafe collapsed beside me on the sofa, sighing heavily as he leaned his head back against a cushion and turned his head to face me.

"I'm sorry."

"I know you are."

"I don't think you're guilty at all."

"I know that too."

"So are you gonna let me defend you without throwing barbed comments my way every two seconds?"

I shrugged. "We'll see," I said, smiling despite myself. I leaned my head against Rafe's as I closed my eyes, not caring about my soaking wet hair dripping on him. When Rafe snaked his arm around my shoulders to pull me in closer, I barely smothered a noise of surprise.

"Five minutes," he mumbled against my cheek. I could feel his breath on my skin as my heart rate rapidly sped up. "We get five minutes like this, and then it's all business. Just five minutes."

"That's longer than we've had in years—are you spoiling me, Rafe Wilde?"

"Shh. Be quiet for once in your life and let us have this."

"You ask for the impossible," I joked quietly, but I dutifully remained quiet, nonetheless.

Neither of us pointed out when our five minutes was blatantly up, nor when it was closer to fifteen minutes or even half an hour. When we were nearing sixty minutes, however, I could feel myself drifting off and knew falling asleep wouldn't be fair to Rafe.

Hating myself for doing so, I broke away from Rafe's embrace, stretching my arms up in the air and yawning as I did.

"Jesus Christ, Kirsten!" Rafe suddenly called out as he pinned me back down to the sofa.

"What?" I asked, confused and excited in equal measure. I had imagined Rafe pinning me down plenty of times, but it had yet to happen in real life. Having the full weight of him on top of me, with his dark eyes boring into my own, was more than I could ever have hoped it would be.

"Your towel was falling down when you stretched," Rafe murmured, his lips way too close to mine for comfort. "Do you have no self-awareness?"

I laughed. "Possibly not."

"You're going to make working together as difficult as humanly possible, aren't you?"

I smiled "...possibly yes? Not intentionally."

Rafe sat up from me, laughing uproariously as I rearranged my towel to preserve some decency. "Not intentionally. Of course. All you need to do is exist in the same physical space as me to make things difficult."

"I guess I could put some clothes on to make it a little easier."

"For the love of God, please do."

I was barely aware of my surroundings as I rushed to my bedroom to throw on a little pair of shorts and an oversized T-shirt I used for pajamas. My heart beat way too fast. I knew my skin must have been flushed as well.

Clearly, Rafe and I couldn't spend an hour together without us both losing our senses entirely.

It wasn't going to be me who made working together difficult for Rafe. The opposite was true as well.

When I returned to Rafe's side on the sofa, he'd pulled out a voice recorder and a notepad.

"I guess it's down to brass tacks now, huh?" I asked, feeling my previous exhaustion return all at once.

Rafe smiled grimly. "Unfortunately so."

He held my gaze, his eyes intent and interested. How I wished for nothing more than to have those eyes never leave mine.

"Now, tell me, Kirsten—what the hell happened last night?"

CHAPTER EIGHT

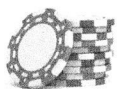

The Collins Vet Clinic was tucked away down a clean, quiet street unadorned with any of the usual trappings of Las Vegas. There were no neon, flashing signs, street performers or drunken idiots. I mean, it was barely noon, but that didn't mean there weren't a fair number of revelers completely and utterly wasted out on the streets already. Time did not exist in Vegas.

I had spent much of Saturday with Kirsten, grilling her on every little piece of information she could provide me with regardless of whether or not she thought it was inconsequential. After the way our day had started, I was worried we wouldn't actually get any work done, but it turned into an incredibly productive meeting.

Kirsten had always been upfront and honest, so she wasn't afraid to divulge information others would be reluctant to give in case it lowered people's opinions of them. We both came from similar backgrounds. She knew I'd understand the context to anything she told me.

At the end of the day, Kirsten wasn't even remotely involved in the charges placed against her. She was just about as separate from mob life as I was. The work that kept her somewhat related to that life was altogether much more legal and safe than the work I'd undertaken. She'd *helped* people. I'd covered up for people.

And therein lay the problem. There may have been someone she helped who wasn't supposed to be helped. Maybe *many* people. My most prevailing theory was that somebody wanted Las Vegas' resident underground mob doctor put away for good.

It was also possible Kirsten had been targeted simply to fray relations between the different mob factions as both Ian and I had originally assumed. I had to work from the angle that it was personal before I explored the idea that it was part of an over-arching plot. Ultimately, the one I was defending was Kirsten. It didn't matter who was actually responsible, be it another person or an entire organization, just so long as I could prove Kirsten was the one who had been framed.

Which meant eventually my meeting with Kirsten came to a fruitless end. She couldn't think of anyone who might have personal grounds to frame her. Luckily, or maybe unluckily for Kirsten, she had few friends. This would make my investigation far quicker than if she were a social butterfly, but I couldn't help feeling a little sad that she lived for her job.

That's precisely where I figured I'd most likely find the answers—at her job. So here I was, standing outside of the Collins Vet Clinic at lunchtime on a Monday, completely reluctant to enter the place.

I knew my hesitancy stemmed from purely personal reasons. Stepping into Kirsten's workplace meant I would find out a lot more about her from her colleagues, and after spending years dutifully trying to ignore each other, I couldn't help feeling like I was invading her privacy. Obviously, that was what I was doing—for the sake of her case—but I worried I'd end up asking questions that were entirely unrelated to defending her as her lawyer.

I sighed heavily. I had to trust my years of education and training as a lawyer. I could be professional. I had to be.

That would have been so much easier to do if Kirsten's boss wasn't Dean Collins.

The man stood by the reception desk when I entered his clinic, sorting out a prescription for a very grumpy-looking cat his receptionist was having trouble with.

"It's an easy mistake to make, Grace, so no worries," he said soothingly. The girl looked as if she had accidentally murdered someone rather than made a work error. "Just double check the measurements on the system. For some things it's in metric, other times imperial; annoying, I know, but hell if I'm going near the program to see if I can change it."

Grace laughed at Dean's comment, which instantly put her at ease. Begrudgingly, I had to admit, what Kirsten had said was right. Her boss really knew how to charm the ladies. Maybe my initial assessment of him being after Kirsten was wrong.

Focus on your bloody job, Rafe, I scolded myself. *Dean's feelings for Kirsten only matter if he had cause to frame her. So...focus.*

It was Rose, entering the reception area from an office, who noticed me first.

"Rafe!" she exclaimed, announcing my presence to Dean, who turned from the desk to smile at me. He looked tired and stressed, but the smile did an excellent job of masking both.

"We were wondering if you would show up today," Dean said, gesturing towards his office. "Kirsten contacted me on Saturday, saying you were defending her. I'm assuming you wish to talk to the staff here?"

I nodded, wondering when Kirsten had contacted the man—I'd stayed pretty late talking with her, and she didn't go near her phone. Were they close enough to be contacting each other in the middle of the night?

"If I could speak to you first, Dr. Collins, that would be great."

"Dean is fine."

Rose regarded the two of us curiously as we entered Dean's office. I wondered why. It was only once the door was closed and the two of us were sitting down that the man spoke again.

"So, Mr. Wilde, was it?"

"Rafe is fine," I replied, echoing Dean's sentiment from earlier.

"Rafe it is, then. Tell me, Rafe, what do you need to know?"

"Everything in an ideal world," I said, earning a chuckle from Dean. "But more specifically, I'm assuming Kirsten has told you what she's been charged with?" Dean nodded. "In which case, my first question would be whether any of your stocks of the following drugs have been lower than expected." I handed Dean a list, but he shook his head before looking at it.

"We're not missing anything," Dean replied. "You think I'd be able to run a legitimate clinic here if I didn't keep track of the most dangerous drugs kept on-site? Don't be ridiculous."

Ah, so the man had a prideful streak. Not unexpected, given how young he was to be running a clinic by himself.

"Do you mind if I ask how old you are?" I ended up wondering aloud. "To be running your own clinic so young—"

He cut through my question with a howl of laughter, running a hand through his hair as he did so.

"I'm really gonna have to take Kirsten's advice to heart and put my I.D. up on the wall, aren't I? Rafe, I'm thirty-nine in a few months. I'm not that young. I inherited this clinic from my uncle. He retired three years ago."

I looked at the man, shocked. I had been sure he was my age. Thirty at an absolute push.

"You sure you're not a vampire? Off the record, of course."

"I'm quite certain I'm not. In any case, our stocks are fine, and Kirsten is being set up. I'm sure you'd worked that out for yourself, though."

"Of course. How informed are you about her...extra clients?" I already knew the answer but had to ask. It would tell me how honest the man was if he was willing to admit to having special clientele.

Dean raised an eyebrow. "I only let her take them on when I'm here. I wouldn't risk her safety—or that of the clinic—for anything. So you could say I'm well-informed."

"Did you ever notice any of these clients holding a grudge against Dr. O'Leary, or did anyone come in looking for a previous client?"

"To the best of my knowledge, no. I'm sure Kirsten would have said the same thing. Nobody comes in here looking for a fight. It's well-known to be neutral ground."

"Does the clinic gain anything from this extra business?"

Dean gave me a wry grin. "Obviously. Not anything worth trying to set Kirsten up to steal, however. You'll notice the street outside is nice and empty. That's about all those clients amount to—safety and cleanliness. I don't take any money from them other than for the supplies Kirsten uses. If she makes a profit from it, then that's her business."

I paused, taking in the information. It was exactly what I'd expected to hear. I decided to change the direction of questioning.

"Did any of these clients seem interested in Dr. O'Leary?"

Dean narrowed his eyes. "Interested how, exactly? Romantically?"

"Yes, or maybe in her capacity as an O'Leary."

"More than a few men who came in did take an interest in Kirsten. She was naturally oblivious, but when the advance was too obvious for even Kirsten to ignore, she always let them down very professionally. There were maybe one or two…"

"Can you give me their names if you know them?"

Dean nodded. "I keep a note of everyone who comes in, so I'll send it over to you with any additional notes I have on each of them."

I was impressed. I hadn't expected Dean to be forthcoming. It struck me that I never should have expected anything less from him.

"Anything else?" he asked politely.

"Er, yes," I said, hating myself for hesitating on the question. But I had to know—both for the case and for personal reasons. "Does your relationship with Dr. O'Leary extend past that of a boss and employee?"

Dean seemed to consider the question for a moment or two as he leaned back against his chair. "We're friends," he eventually said. "We get on very well. Other than the occasional lunch outside of the office, our relationship is largely professional. Friday night at Capone's was actually the first time any of us in the clinic had socialized together at night. We all keep very hectic work schedules as you might expect."

I stopped myself from breathing an obvious sigh of relief. Kirsten had been right, there *was* nothing going on. Ian had clearly planted the idea in my head to mess with me. What a dick. Silently promising to get him back for that, I stood up and shook Dean's hand as he did the same.

"Thank you very much for your time, Dean. If it's all right with you, I'd like to question Rose West, and then I'll be out of your hair."

Dean smiled. "Take all the time you need."

When we re-entered the reception area, it became immediately apparent both Rose and Grace had been trying to eavesdrop. I only just managed to hide a smirk.

"Rose, you can take Rafe's questions in the kitchen," Dean said, prompting Rose to leap out of her seat behind the reception desk to lead me through to the kitchen.

"Oh my God, is Kirsten okay? She didn't say much on the phone. I can't imagine what that holding cell must have been like. Oh my God, I couldn't do that, I—"

"Rose," I interrupted, causing the woman to shut up immediately. She smiled bashfully.

"Sorry, I was just letting all my thoughts out at once. Is she okay?"

"Dr. O'Leary is doing much better now that she's back at her apartment. Although, she wishes she didn't have to avoid the clinic."

Rose pouted. "It sucks. She's basically my only friend here. I hope this gets sorted soon."

"Do you have any idea who might be responsible for

framing Dr. O'Leary?"

"I wish I could be more helpful, but honestly, I'm not around much when her other clients visit. There are a couple who are in quite a lot, but I think they're in more frequently just to see her, if you know what I mean—"

"Can I get their names?" I asked, wondering if they'd match up with Dean's list.

Rose looked up at the ceiling as she bit her lip in thought. I couldn't help thinking of how endearing she was. I was glad Kirsten had her as a friend.

"I don't remember all their names, but I can give you what I know. I'm pretty good with faces and accents though, so I can describe the ones I don't know by name."

"That would be excellent. If you could send that to me, that would be ideal."

Rose grinned. "Anything I can do to help."

I paused before my next question. "Is there anyone else who may have been interested in Kirsten or had been spurned by her in the past? Like, any of her *actual* clients or—"

"What, you mean other than Dean?" Rose interrupted, catching me off-guard.

"Dr. O'Leary turned him down?"

She sucked on her lip. "Not exactly. Well, see, I'd just started at the clinic about six months ago, so Kirsten had already been here for half a year as a junior vet. I think she also did some work here during her final year at college. So, anyway…I assumed she and Dean had a thing going by the way they acted. I wasn't close to Kirsten at the time, so I just...asked Dean about it instead. He said he'd made his interest in Kirsten pretty clear during her clinical trials and asked her out on a date when she started working here for real. Classic Kirsten, she didn't think he was serious."

"Why was that?"

"Well, she assumed he just wanted to mentor her or whatever. She thought he wouldn't be interested in someone that much younger than him. Now, having met you, I get why she's so oblivious. She obviously can't think of anyone else as dating material with you on her mind."

I didn't quite know how to take this deluge of information. So Dean had asked Kirsten out before. That didn't mean he still liked her romantically. It had nothing to do with the case since he clearly wouldn't try to frame Kirsten either way.

On a personal level, knowing Kirsten's feelings for me prevented her from going out with anyone else both pleased me and made me incredibly sad.

We were toxic for each other. Our attraction had prevented us from moving on. So why couldn't we shake our feelings?

I stood up. "Thanks, Rose, that's everything for now. Please send me anything you know about Dr. O'Leary's evening clients as soon as you can."

She smiled. "Anything you need, Rafe."

I left the Collins Veterinary Clinic with more questions raised than answers given.

I had a sinking feeling in the pit of my stomach that this case, and my feelings for Kirsten, were going to take a long time to sort out.

CHAPTER NINE

Dean was late. Or I was early. Checking my phone for the time, I realized it was the latter—I was painfully early.

But who could blame me? I no longer had a job to go to. I couldn't leave the city or go out at night.

Being accused of a crime I didn't commit sucked.

And so here I was, sitting in a pancake house fifteen minutes early, having actually gotten there twenty-five minutes early. I sighed heavily. What an idiot I was, but I needed to get out of my apartment. Not the least because I felt like a prisoner within my own home. Sure, I could have visited the family home and stayed there for a few days, but something was stopping me.

If this whole set-up was a plot to involve the Irish mob in something, then I didn't want to give anyone a reason to believe I suspected as much. I needed to keep up the front that I was independent and wasn't going to run to my daddy or big brothers for help. I could only hope it was the right move.

The other reason I wanted out of my apartment was that I kept thinking of Rafe pinning me down beneath him on the sofa while I was dressed in nothing but a towel. Even though nothing had happened, the tension had remained. I doubted it was going to disappear any time soon.

It wasn't just the sexual tension. When we'd leaned against each other for the best part of an hour, saying and doing nothing, I'd been overcome with an overwhelming peace—a sense of rightness that had been missing from my life. I didn't think I'd been as relaxed as that in a long, long time—not since Rafe and I stopped speaking to each other. It had felt like a fundamental part of my life had finally been returned to me.

That wasn't fair because I knew Rafe had only taken this case out of duty to me. He knew I couldn't turn to anyone else. Once my name was cleared, he'd go back to his life outside of the mob and I would have to let him. Even if I myself wanted out.

And yet…

There was a small, desperate part of me that hoped this case, alongside Matt and Katya's marriage, would help bridge the gap between the Irish, Italian, and Russian mobs. For all intents and purposes, the Wildes were out of the game, which meant the main players were my father and the new Russian head, Sergei Volkov. Anyone might be trying to topple them, be they a member of the new Colombian faction or from within their own syndicates.

"God, I needed to get out of this shit for real," I muttered into my soda.

"I don't doubt you do," came a voice from behind, startling me half out of my skin.

"Christ, Dean, don't do that to me," I exclaimed as the man sat down opposite me, grinning like a maniac at my fright. "You're early."

He raised an eyebrow. "You're earlier."

"Touché."

He looked tired, and for what felt like the first time, older than thirty. When Dean noticed I was watching him, he frowned.

"You look like you're expecting me to keel over."

"Well, you are covering most of my shifts."

"As if you need to remind me. And it's only Thursday—of week one. I seriously think I'm going to have to hire some temporary cover."

I couldn't help balking at that—someone taking over my job? I couldn't take it.

"I wish I could come back to work," I said quietly, head drooped. A curled finger under my chin surprised me as Dean gently lifted my head up.

"That childhood friend of yours is going to clear your name, Kirsten O'Leary, and then you'll be back at work before you know it. I'll give you some of my shifts, too, just to see how you like it."

God, Dean always knew what to say to make me laugh—something I felt like I hadn't been able to do in days.

"So you don't suspect for even a second that I'm guilty of the crimes I'm being charged with?" I asked.

He shook his head, chuckling slightly. "Not even for a second. You don't have it in you to be a criminal."

"What, not even a little bit? My family background didn't give you pause for even one second when you employed me?"

"It wasn't your family background that gave me pause when deciding to hire you, no."

"How reassuring—wait, something else gave you pause?"

"Ah, that's the waiter now. Are you ready to order?" he asked, clearly deflecting my question. "I'll have the double stack with maple syrup, whipped cream and vanilla ice cream, please," he told the waiter, eliciting an incredulous look from me. Dean shrugged his shoulders. "I have a long afternoon ahead of me. I need the sugar."

"I'll have a regular stack with bacon and maple syrup, please," I told the waiter, then returned to staring at Dean.

"What?"

"What gave you pause when hiring me after I finished college? Not to sound arrogant, but I figured I was a pretty great student."

"You were—and are. It had nothing to do with either your academic or family background."

"So what was it?"

"You're not going to let this go, are you?" He looked—

reluctant. It only made me want to know the answer even more.

"Have I ever let something go before?"

"Not to the best of my knowledge. You know we wouldn't be having this conversation if you weren't so oblivious, Kirsten."

"And what's that supposed to mean?"

"I asked you out. Like, four times."

I stared at him, stunned to silence. What the hell was he talking about?

I tilted my head in confusion. "Excuse me?" I finally said.

Dean rolled his eyes in exasperation.

"See, this is what I mean. I asked you out three times in your final placement, then risked it and asked again when I finally hired you. The first three rejections I willfully dismissed since you were busy being a stressed final-year student who could barely tell her elbow from her knee. I wasn't sure if I could handle having you as a full-time employee, but you were too good a vet for me to pass up hiring you. I figured it was worth asking you out one, final time, but…"

"But?"

"You joked you were young enough to be my daughter, and you figured I was asking you out to give you sage life advice."

"I—oh. I remember that. You were asking me out?"

"How are you so smart and this dense, O'Leary?"

"I'm not dense," I bit out with a strong dose of irritation. "Clearly, you didn't make your feelings obvious enough."

He laughed at that. "Kirsten, both Rose and Grace have known about my feelings for you for months. Even the part-time veterinary nurse we had in over winter clocked onto it. I didn't have to say a word about it to them, they all worked it out by watching us."

Oh. I didn't really have anything to say to that. Had my head really been so full of pining for Rafe that I had frozen out any guy who showed the slightest interest?

Dean? My boss, Dean Collins, had feelings for me. It just seemed…ridiculous.

"You flirt with anything on two legs, sometimes more," I said, thinking of the way he crooned at the pets brought into the clinic, much to the delight of our female (and sometimes male) clients.

"And? Since when has liking someone meant you can't flirt? Especially when the person you like is as block-headed as you are."

I reached across the table and poked his shoulder. "See, now you're just insulting me. How am I supposed to like you back if all you do is make fun of me?"

"So all I have to do is dial it back on the insults, and you'll like me? God, had I only known that from the beginning."

I couldn't help laughing.

"I don't mind the insults, really. Do you seriously like me?"

He gave me a small, very genuine smile that did strange things to my stomach.

"Yes, seriously. Now that you know, will you give my feelings some thought? It's not as if you've got much going on to preoccupy you right now, anyway."

"You're such a dick," I threw back at him, and then, "yes, seriously. I'll think about your feelings."

I couldn't keep pining after Rafe. It was time to move on. Whether that meant with Dean or someone else further down the line, who knew? I just knew it had to happen.

"Ah, I didn't realize I was going to interrupt such a *serious* conversation," a voice suddenly said, and I turned in horror. Why the hell was *Rafe* here?

"Rafe, what are you—why are you—"

"Dr. Collins had some files he needed to hand over to me, so he asked me to meet him here on his lunch break. I got here way too early, so I figured I'd grab some food, but luckily for me, he's already here."

"Rafe," Dean said mildly, inclining his head before rummaging through his bag and retrieving the documents he needed to hand over.

I couldn't move, couldn't speak. How much had Rafe heard? Clearly enough to warrant that tumultuous expression on his face.

"Well, I don't want to interrupt your date, so I'll be moving along. I'll see you tomorrow at ten, Kirsten," Rafe muttered before hurrying away.

He was out of sight before I regained the ability to speak.

"You didn't want him to hear any of that, did you?" Dean asked, observant as usual.

"No," I replied honestly.

"He's the one you're hung up on."

"Yes."

I didn't know how I expected Dean to react, but a nonchalant shrug of the shoulders was certainly not even an option that crossed my mind.

"At least now I know you have great standards. It's only worth having a love rival if they're not a complete idiot, I guess."

"What?"

"I was worried the guy you were hung up on was going to be a complete and utter, hopeless mobster. I'd never be able to compete with someone I didn't understand. Him, on the other hand," Dean gestured outside towards the road Rafe had disappeared down, "him, I can understand. That works for me."

When our pancakes finally arrived, he easily turned our conversation back to tales of the vet clinic, of Rose missing her boyfriend, and of Grace only now taking an interest in the goings-on of her fellow workmates because of my arrest. When we finally paid the bill, I couldn't, in all honesty, remember anything that was said.

"Look after yourself, O'Leary," Dean said when we left the pancake house and reached the crossroads where our paths split. "If you think of any information you might need from us, just let me know."

"Thanks, Dean."

Then he leaned in, and for a moment I thought he would kiss me. Then he sighed and pulled me into a hug instead.

"Don't dwell on things too much. Just put yourself first and sort out this arrest before you deal with anything else."

"I will. Now get back to the clinic before Rose complains that you've cut into her lunch hour."

Dean left, leaving me to do exactly what he told me not to do. I returned to my apartment, to dwell on everything both Dean and Rafe had said. *And hadn't said*, I thought bitterly.

Frustrated at the lot life was currently dealing me, the clock hands had barely hit five in the evening before I headed over to my liquor cabinet and pulled out an unopened bottle of a twelve-year Red Breast whiskey. I hadn't been one for the stuff a few years ago, but I'd developed a taste for it lately.

Guess that means I'm finally living up to my Irish roots.

I should have known that, two hours later, I'd end up at the door of the Wilde estate, banging on the wood in a drunken uproar. I knew it was stupid, but I didn't care.

CHAPTER TEN

I knew who it was pounding on the door before I opened it—and not just because the Wilde mansion had video security. I seriously considered not opening the door. I didn't want to after the conversation I'd overheard between Kirsten and Dean. Who could blame me? And yet, I opened the door.

"I brought booze," Kirsten said, holding up a bottle of whiskey and swirling the contents as she did. It was clear she'd already helped herself to some alcohol if her frenetic energy and dilated pupils were anything to go by.

"Clearly."

"Aren't you going to let me in? You are my lawyer, after all. You can't say no."

"Considering it's after office hours, I'd say I can," I replied, though I moved aside and let Kirsten in nonetheless, following her along the hallway that led to the kitchen or the ground floor living room. When Kirsten headed toward the stairs, I grabbed her wrist without thinking. "Where are you going?"

She looked at me as if it were obvious. Her green eyes glittered with amusement in the low light of the hallway. "To your bedroom—where else?"

I ran a hand over my face. "Kirsten, what are you doing? Why are you doing this? It isn't professional."

"Neither was the way you spoke to me and Dean earlier," she hit back immediately, which was true. "But I'm not here to complain. I'm here to clear the air. So drink with me."

"But why in my bedroom?"

Kirsten glanced down towards the living room. "The rooms down here are too big for two people. And besides, your bedroom reminds me of good old times, playing board games and doing our homework and sneaking our first few beers together."

Her comment made me laugh despite myself, and then Kirsten knew she'd won. It always struck me as odd that our families were at war and somehow we'd found peace. While my father didn't like her presence, he did like to rub her visits in Liam's face every time he got a chance.

"Head on up, then," I said, "I'll grab a couple glasses."

"Glasses? Very classy, Rafe."

"We don't all want to swig from the bottle as much as you do."

"Blame Ian for that."

"I know. Now go on up."

I made a stop in the ground floor bathroom first and checked my appearance in the mirror. My hair was a little longer than I usually let it grow, but it had been swept away from my face for work for so long, I'd simply forgotten to get it cut. Now, free of product after the shower I'd only gotten out of half an hour ago, the top of my hair fell over my forehead—some of it was almost touching my eyes.

It made me look younger. It made me feel nostalgic.

Nostalgic if I ignored the shadows under my eyes that gave away my tired and stressful career. How could it be that Kirsten's eyes hadn't darkened from stress, too? She seemed ageless somehow, despite the fact that she was easily under as much stress as I was on a regular basis. She was beautiful, with her red-brown hair and flawless skin, punctuated with a tiny spray of freckles across her nose that only made her more stunning.

And those eyes. They were nothing like my dark ones, which were currently boring through the mirror right back at me. Kirsten was all lightness and laughter and saving stray kittens and secret plots to prank our brothers. I was the moody, quiet one she forced out of his shell years ago. I might not have become the person I was if not for Kirsten O'Leary.

That was why it stung so damn much that I might actually have lost her to Dean. I sighed at my reflection. If that was what Kirsten had come to tell me, it was time for me to take it like a man.

Stopping only to grab two glasses from the kitchen, I made

my way up the stairs to my bedroom, where Kirsten lay on my bed—waiting—for me.

She was lying on my bed. This woman was impossible.

"What? Was the giant sofa in front of the bay window not enough for you, O'Leary?" I mused as I pushed Kirsten over enough for me to sit on the bed beside her. She skillfully poured a stream of whiskey into the two glasses in my hand. I promptly downed the contents of one of the glasses before filling it up again.

"Clearly, I was right to come over with booze." Kirsten laughed as she continued to swig whiskey from the bottle despite having a glass of the stuff in her other hand.

"Yes, because alcohol is never a bad idea."

"You certainly don't seem to think so right now if the rate you're drinking the stuff is anything to go by."

"On the contrary," I mused, "it's because it's a terrible idea I'm drinking."

Kirsten clinked her glass with mine. "I'll drink to that."

There was silence for a few minutes as the two of us drank more whiskey. Watching Kirsten out of the corner of my eye, I could tell she was waiting for me to speak.

Guess it's time to ask, then.

"So…you and Dean are a real thing now?"

Kirsten almost spat out her drink. "Christ almighty, you jump to conclusions pretty quickly, don't you?"

"What do you mean?"

"Dean did say he liked me, yeah. And I admit, I can't believe I didn't notice it before—"

"Kirsten, Ian and I noticed it within two seconds. How unaware can you be?"

"And whose fault do you think that is?"

"What the hell do you mean?"

Kirsten turned to face me, her expression fierce.

"The only reason I never noticed Dean's feelings was that I was too involved in my feelings for you," she said, jabbing a finger into my chest as she did. "But we're not 'allowed' to be together, so of course I've got to try to move on. Why else do you think I'd tell him I'd consider his feelings?"

"So you're going to—"

"My God, why do you always hear one thing I say and assume it means another, Rafe? I'm not going out with him. I said I'd think about it at some point after all this shit-storm of a drug bust is over. And he was the one who said I had to think about myself first, not me. That's how conscientious he is… unlike someone else I know."

"If I'm so awful, then why do you like me so much?" I knew I sounded like a child, but I couldn't help it. I was jealous, plain and simple.

Kirsten saw right through me. I realized far too late she could tell and half the reason she'd said anything to me this evening was to bait me into showing my true feelings.

Kirsten smirked. "Unlike with anyone else, Rafe Wilde, I know what you think of me. I don't need anybody else to point it out. That's why the only way we could hide our feelings was to literally ignore one another for four years, but I'm done with that."

"Is that so?" I asked, downing another glass of whiskey in the process. I could tell where this was going—could tell I had to stop it—but not a single bone in my body wanted to.

Kirsten was sitting in front of me, gorgeous even in a zip-up hoodie and shorts, her full bottom lip caught between her teeth as she looked at me. I imagined tasting the whiskey on those lips, and before I knew it, I could feel a roiling heat down beneath my stomach that had nothing to do with the alcohol.

Kirsten leaned in closer to me. "Don't look at me like this is a mistake, Rafe," she murmured, so close to my lips that I'd barely have to move to kiss them. "How could two people who have wanted each other for this long be a mistake?"

I didn't know if it was because of the alcohol or because of my deep-seated feelings for Kirsten or frustration—or all three of the above—but I completely agreed with her. Wanting Kirsten could never be a mistake.

She barely had a second's notice before I snaked a hand through her hair and closed the gap between us, crushing her lips beneath mine and finally tasting the whiskey upon them.

I was sure to regret this in the morning, but right now I didn't care.

CHAPTER ELEVEN

It felt like I was dreaming. Or maybe it was the alcohol… maybe both. Probably both. But Rafe Wilde was kissing me. And damn, was he good at it. How many years had I imagined this? It felt far longer than I could remember.

I ran a hand through Rafe's hair as he was doing to mine, pulling him in closer, closer, closer. But it wasn't enough. I wanted more. Funny how things happened like that—I finally got to fulfill my dream of kissing the guy I'd been pining after for most of my life, and it was suddenly, abruptly inadequate.

I wanted to see our clothes littering the floor, ripped off our bodies in reckless abandon in our desperation for each other.

Well. No time like the present.

My hand drifted from Rafe's hair down over his grey T-shirt, snaking underneath the hem to allow my fingers to explore the planes of his body unencumbered. His skin was smooth, his body sculpted. This was the body of a man who took care of himself. The fire that had been building inside me all evening flared up. I wanted Rafe. I wanted him more than anything, and I needed him to know that.

"Rafe…" I murmured against his lips. He circled one of his arms around my waist as he set me down on the bed and lay on top of me, his fingers making quick work of the zipper on my hoodie. With a shrug, I threw the garment off, then slid Rafe's T-shirt up and over his head, throwing it unceremoniously to the floor.

We were really going to do this. I thought my heart might burst with excitement.

"I wish I could quit you," Rafe said quietly, his voice rough and unsteady as he broke away from my lips to glance downwards, his eyebrows raised. I don't think he'd expected me to have nothing but a bra on underneath my hoodie, leaving me exposed now that he'd removed it.

I reached up and bit his upper lip. "No, you don't. Other people want that for you. Not you."

"Why are you always right, Kirsten?"

"It's a gift. You should really listen to me more. But…"

"But?"

I gave Rafe a wicked grin. "Talking and listening isn't what I want to do right now."

Rafe matched my grin before kissing me again with

renewed fervor, the skin-on-skin contact from removing the top half of our clothes made me all the more desperate for the man on top of me. I could feel him rock hard, against my leg. I bucked up into him, causing Rafe to moan slightly.

"Kirsten..."

I ran my fingers underneath the waistband of the sweatpants he wore, wishing they were already off. I needed Rafe in me. I needed—

"Kirsten." Rafe's voice was louder now. More insistent. Reluctantly, I looked up at him, knowing I wouldn't like the expression on his face. I was right.

"Don't tell me to stop, Rafe," I pleaded. "Don't you dare."

"We can't do this. We can't."

I wriggled free of him to sit up on the bed, feeling my face heat up in anger and shame.

"Even now, going this far, you still can't? What the hell has to change for you to man the hell up and just be with me like you want?"

"Kirsten, I'm your lawyer! Ignoring everything else, I'm your lawyer. Surely, you can see how this is problematic? If the detective and court catch even a hint of this attraction between the two of us, they'll have cause to throw the entire case I'm building for you under the proverbial bus. And I can't see you go to prison. I won't."

I stared at Rafe, speechless—how was it this had completely escaped me? I'd been so involved in my own feelings, I hadn't considered what this would do to Rafe's career —or to my freedom.

How was it possible to be so self-absorbed, I could actually ruin my own life?

And still, I wanted him. Tears stung my eyes, threatening to escape, but I didn't care.

"Rafe, I lo—"

"Don't do this, Kirsten. Please."

"Rafe!"

"Wait until I've cleared your name," he roared back, causing me to recoil. "You know how I feel about you. You've got to realize how hard this is on me, too, but we've got to do the right thing. You know we do."

I knew he was right, but I didn't want to accept it. I ran my hands through my hair, frantic. I didn't want to have to think about our families and the mob and this stupid set-up of a case against me. I just wanted to be with him. I lowered my head, staring at my knees but seeing nothing.

"Run away with me."

I knew he was frowning at me even though I couldn't see it. "What did you just say?" he asked quietly.

I threw my head up to stare at him. "Run away with me. Screw that I can't leave Vegas. If this whole drug thing against me is a set-up, I'm probably in danger anyway." It was so easy to believe what I was saying when it was at least partially true. I continued. "You can practice law anywhere. The same for me and veterinary medicine. So let's leave."

Rafe said nothing for a few moments. "Are you serious?"

"Yes."

"Really serious?"

"Yes."

Rafe looked away and laughed a little crazily, then he picked his T-shirt up off the floor and flung my hoodie at me. "Then screw it, let's do it."

Wait. What? "Y-you're okay with this?"

Rafe pulled his T-shirt back on before wandering around his room, flinging clothes and miscellaneous items into a small bag.

"You're right, Kirsten. If this was a set-up and it's mob related, then there's no promise this won't happen again to you in the future. We both want out of this stupid life, so let's just…do it."

My excitement from earlier started bubbling up again, this time for entirely different reasons.

"I need to grab some stuff from my apartment."

"That's no problem. We'll swing by there first, then we'll get the hell out of Vegas."

Clearly, Rafe was ignoring the fact that we'd both been drinking. I was fine with that. We were allowed to be reckless. It was about time we were reckless.

When I stood up and re-zipped my hoodie, Rafe surprised me by picking me up and spinning me around, kissing me as I laughed in surprise.

"Ian is gonna be pissed," Rafe joked, "and he'll be the least of our worries."

"Eloping wouldn't be eloping if you weren't running away from at least a couple of problems."

"I guess you're right." Rafe kissed my forehead, then put me back on my feet. Taking my hand in his, he led me out of his room, down the stairs, across the hallway, and into the adjoining garage. It was a huge space, full of expensive, vintage sports cars. But Rafe took me over to a car that stood out by virtue of it being a 'normal' car—a red Audi Quattro.

Rafe gave me a meaningful glance. "I think this has always been here as an emergency getaway car. Boring and not ostentatious in the slightest."

"I actually like them, to be honest," I said with a small smile. "They're pretty nice cars."

Rafe laughed. "Of course you have cheap taste in cars."

"As long as it will take me from A to B without falling apart, it's fine by me."

I could almost hear the pounding of Rafe's heart in the darkness of the garage. It matched the tempo of mine. With a flick of a switch, the garage doors opened and Rafe threw his bag into the back seat, opening the passenger door to let me in before sliding over the hood to reach the driver's side.

"Smooth," I said as he started up the engine.

"I may have practiced that a few times as a teen to impress you. I somehow never got to do it in front of you though."

"Absolutely tragic."

He revved the engine, moved the car into first gear, and then we were gone.

We were really doing this. We were going to leave Las Vegas.

The drive over to my apartment was possibly the most exciting drive I'd ever experienced. Certainly the most liberating. The two of us were laughing, singing along to rock music on the radio and sneaking kisses every time we had to stop at a red light.

I felt like we were ten years younger than we actually were, starting our relationship for real in our teens like we should have been able to. We had so much lost time to make up for.

Running away no longer seemed like a stupid, fanciful escape—it was the right thing to do. Rafe and I belonged together. If that was a problem for anyone else…well. Soon, they'd no longer be a problem for us.

I spared a moment's thought for Dean, who in reality didn't wish either Rafe or me any harm. I knew if I told him I loved Rafe and it would be unfair to try to reciprocate his feelings, he would understand. He was a good guy.

It made me feel just a tiny bit guilty we were leaving without so much as a word of warning to anyone. That feeling was gone almost as soon as I felt it. Rafe and I had to do what was right for us.

In a haze of excitement and residual alcohol, we reached my apartment before I was ready to get there. I was almost tempted to tell Rafe to continue driving—I could buy clothes and anything else I needed anywhere. But I had important things in my apartment I really needed to pick up. My passport, I.D., savings account details, and a framed photo of my mother and me. It was the only one in my possession—the one thing I could never replace.

I resisted the urge to tell Rafe to drive on, and he slowed the Audi to a halt in front of my apartment building. I turned to face him, smiling before planting a kiss on his lips.

"As soon as we're out of Vegas, you can bet your ass we're continuing where we left off in your bedroom, Rafe."

"I'd be extremely disappointed if we didn't."

I laughed. "Great. Now that we have that established, I won't be inside long. Like, less than five minutes, so stay out here in the car with the engine running so I really feel like I'm escaping in the middle of the night."

"Kirsten, it's barely eight."

I rolled my eyes. "You get what I mean, spoilsport," he responded by ruffling my hair.

"Don't take long. And remember to pack some leggings or something—you're gonna get cold in those shorts pretty fast."

"Yes, Dad."

Rafe winced. "I don't think I'm into the daddy kink, so maybe lay off that."

"You're such a weirdo when you try to stop acting like a super-serious grown up."

Rafe waved a hand toward my apartment impatiently. "Go get your stu—"

I glanced at him, confused as to why he would stop mid-sentence. "Rafe?" I wondered aloud.

He scowled. "You didn't leave a light on when you left your apartment, did you, Kirsten?"

I shook my head, then, turning to face my apartment building, realized what Rafe saw. My living room light was on.

I looked at him. Both of us sobered up and were brought back to reality by that one, single light. A cold wave of fear washed up my spine.

"Someone's in my apartment."

CHAPTER TWELVE

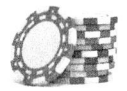

"You are not going up there alone, Kirsten."

"Obviously not. You're coming up with me."

"We should probably call the police."

"I somehow doubt they'll arrive in time to catch whoever's in there," she replied, her tone dry and sarcastic. "I especially doubt they'll respond to a call from someone they believe to be a criminal."

Whether she was right or not, if she didn't want to call the police, then that was up to her. "The two of us it is, then," I said, getting out of the Audi at the same time Kirsten did. "Just don't do anything reckless."

"Me, reckless? I have no clue what you're talking about."

"Very funny. Now, get behind me."

She thankfully followed my command without complaint,

wordlessly handing over her keys to the building and her apartment. I had to admit, even I felt nervous—if someone really was in Kirsten's apartment, then it was unlikely going to be a good thing. If the intruder was armed, well...

All I had were my fists. The best I could hope for was the element of surprise or that the intruder was here to plant evidence rather than hurt anyone.

Imagine a lawyer hoping someone is actually planting evidence. I'm in way over my head.

I meant that in more ways than one. I was only a newly graduated lawyer, after all—it didn't matter that I'd been at the top of my class or the only one Kirsten could trust to defend her. At the end of the day, I wasn't entirely convinced I could find a way to win her case, not with so little to work with.

That was part of the reason why running off with Kirsten had been such an appealing idea. If I didn't—or couldn't—win her case, then she would go to prison. I'd meant what I said earlier. I wouldn't be able to cope with that, never mind the fact that Kirsten didn't deserve to go to prison in the first place.

And she had been correct, of course. If this was mob-related (which it almost definitely was), then there was no guarantee she wouldn't be set up again. Or, for that matter, me. Getting out of Vegas was what was best for both of us.

If only we'd done it years ago.

But now we had to deal with what was right in front of us, no matter how unpleasant or frightening that might be.

We soundlessly navigated the hallways and stairs to the second floor. It almost felt as if Kirsten wasn't daring to breathe. I couldn't blame her; I felt much the same way, and it wasn't even my apartment that had been broken into.

Kirsten's front door lying open was all the confirmation we needed that there was definitely someone inside her apartment. Shifting her further behind me with my arm, I took several purposeful steps inside.

"Whoever the hell is in here, get out right now," I bellowed. There was a moment of silence, followed by the sound of smashing glass, then a masked man came hurtling out of Kirsten's bedroom, pushed past me with all his weight and threw Kirsten against the wall as he made his escape.

I ran after him, but he vaulted over the stairway guardrail and was outside before I'd made it down a single flight. When I returned to Kirsten's side, she was picking herself up off the floor. The poor thing was shaking.

"Kirsten, he didn't hurt you, did he?" I asked, torn between worry and fury.

"N-no," she stammered, "but he's done a number on m-my apartment."

Kirsten was right. Taking a look around the place, I realized the intruder had upturned or ripped into just about every piece of furniture she possessed. Her kitchen and bathroom hadn't fared much better when I wandered over to inspect them. A wracked sob coming from the bedroom had me bolting over to the sound in a second.

I found Kirsten sitting on the floor, surrounded by shards of glass and clutching an empty picture frame. She looked at me with eyes full of tears.

"He took it."

"What did he take?" I asked as I gently swept the glass away from the floor. Some shards had cut her knees open, but Kirsten didn't seem to notice.

"The photo of me and my mother. It was the only one I had. And he—he took it."

My mind was blank. Why would the intruder have taken a photo of Kirsten and her mother?

I coaxed her onto her feet and over to the bed. Though the duvet was torn to shreds and the mattress was in tatters, it was still preferable to sitting in a pile of broken glass.

"It's okay, sweetheart. There must be other photos of your mother."

"That's the thing—this is the only one of me with her!" Kirsten wailed, tears streaming unchecked down her face.

"Surely, your father must have—"

"There was that small fire when I was eleven, remember?" Kirsten cut in.

I did vaguely recall us having conspired to work out who had started that fire, though, in all honesty, I couldn't remember if the culprit had ever been discovered.

"What about the fire?" I asked, gaining an inkling of what she was about to say.

"It was in my father's study, where he kept all the family photos. Everything was destroyed. All that remained were a handful of photos of my mom and dad when they got married and on their honeymoon, one of my mom with Patrick and Ian, and...this one. And now it's gone."

I was speechless. It felt too much to be a coincidence that the intruder just so happened to know this was her only surviving photo of herself with her mother. They had to have known, but now wasn't the time to say that.

I sat beside her, hugging her tightly as I stroked her hair. "You'll be okay. Shh, don't cry. We're gonna work this out." I paused, then added quietly, "Sweetheart, I need to call the police."

"I know," she mumbled against my chest, voice choked with tears. "I know."

"I'm gonna call now, then I'll sort out those knees. They're a mess."

Kirsten looked down at her legs as if only just noticing they were bleeding. She winced. "Shit, I didn't—I didn't realize."

"It's okay. Just stay there. I'll be back in a moment."

Fifteen minutes later, Kirsten was cleaned up and the police had arrived. After explaining what had happened to the detective—Charles Peters, who was the detective taking charge of Kirsten's entire drug case—I exited out into the hallway to call Ian.

No number of deep breaths was going to be able to prepare me for this conversation, but Ian had to know. Kirsten's entire family had to know.

The phone rang once, twice. By the third ring, I was ready

to hang up and simply drive Kirsten over to her family home, but then Ian picked up.

"Rafe? What's up? Can't wait until tomorrow for a drink? I feel you, man—"

"Someone broke into your sister's apartment."

The silence on the other end of the line was somber and serious.

"Is she okay?" was all he asked.

"Shaken up. Scared shitless. Cut herself on some glass, and the asshole pushed her into the wall when he left—"

"Wait, she was there when it happened?"

"No, she—we—got to her apartment, and the light was on. The guy got spooked and ran out when we confronted him."

"Jesus Christ, Rafe. I'm coming over. I'll be ten minutes, tops."

Ian made the journey in seven. The second he saw Kirsten, he wrapped her up in his arms and she started sobbing all over again.

"This place is a mess, huh? At least you weren't inside when the guy broke in," Ian murmured, using his usual mix of sincerity hidden behind sarcasm to calm her down.

"Ian, they—they took the photo of me and Mom."

The change in Ian's expression when he heard that was entirely unexpected. He froze, but she was too buried against him to see it.

I did.

Ian glared at me as if to say 'We can talk about this later, but don't you dare ask about it now.' I was smart enough to take that advice.

"Kirsten," Ian continued, "finish giving your statement to the detective, and I'll take you home." He looked at me. "Do you need a lift, too, Rafe? I didn't see your car out there."

"Ah, I took the Audi," I said, realizing too late Ian knew about the Quattro. He knew what it meant.

My best friend frowned at me. "Come in my car anyway, and we can talk at the house once Kirsten's in bed."

"I'm not a child, Ian," Kirsten mumbled.

"You'll always be my kid sister, though. Go speak to Detective what's-his-name, and we'll be off."

When she reluctantly left the two of us to speak to Detective Peters, Ian full-on glared at me.

"What the hell were you planning, you son of a bitch?" he growled.

But I'd had enough. I stood my ground.

"Just…don't, Ian. Don't test me. Kirsten and I are consenting adults—"

"She's my sister."

"And? She's an adult. We were planning to leave together. We knew what the consequences were, but look at what we literally just walked in on. Kirsten isn't safe in Vegas."

"She's isn't safe here, definitely. That's why she's going to stay at home."

"Ian, I don't think that's a good idea. If this is a ploy to get to your entire family—"

"Then we'll deal with it as a family," Ian all but spat out. "You're Kirsten's lawyer. All you're supposed to do is clear her name of this drug charge. You're not responsible for anything else, no matter how much you try to prove otherwise."

Oh. That hurt. Just as I was about to respond, Detective Peters and Kirsten returned.

"I have all I need, for now, Mr. Wilde. Mr. O'Leary," the man said, looking at the two of us in turn. "You'll need to vacate the premises so we can do a full sweep and determine if this is related to the charges placed against Dr. O'Leary—"

"They're obviously connected," Ian burst out.

Peters sighed. "I'm not at liberty to come to such a conclusion at this moment." He inclined his head at me. "Mr. Wilde, might I have a word with you tomorrow?"

I nodded, curious but confused. "Of course."

"Then all of you are free to go," he glanced at Kirsten, "provided you're taking Dr. O'Leary to her family home." We all nodded.

With everything going on, I had almost forgotten Kirsten had her freedom restricted. It felt like a lifetime ago that we'd foolishly decided to run from our problems.

I wish we'd never stopped by her apartment, but it was too late now.

When I went to wrap my arm around her shoulders, Ian pushed me subtly but unceremoniously out of the way to wrap his arm around her himself. He ushered his sister into the front passenger seat, leaving me to sit in the back of his car.

The drive to the O'Leary house was the polar opposite of mine and Kirsten's drive earlier. Silent. Serious. Scary.

For what felt like the hundredth time, I had to wonder, *What the hell is going on?*

And who the hell is after Kirsten?

CHAPTER THIRTEEN

I barely remembered getting home from my apartment. I felt numb, aside from the stinging in my knees where I'd cut them on the glass on my bedroom floor.

Someone had broken in and trashed my apartment. I didn't even know what they were looking for, or if it had merely served to scare me shitless. What would have happened had I been in, alone? Was the only reason my apartment was broken into because I hadn't been in at the time, or had the intention been to harm me if I'd been there?

And on top of all that…they took the one photo that existed of my mother and me. Tiny, newborn Kirsten O'Leary, wrapped in her mother's tired and happy arms, just hours before she suffered the fatal aneurysm that stole her from my family forever. Thinking about it caused a few errant tears to escape my eyes.

Those few hours in the hospital were all I got with my mother. I never got to know her. Never got to spend any time with her. And yet, I loved her fiercely and grew up on stories about her from my father and brothers and everyone else who knew her. Every day, I looked at my life and wondered if I'd grown up to be a woman my mother could be proud of. I hoped I was.

The intruder must have known about the importance of that photo, otherwise, why would he have taken it? Even if the only point of taking the photo was to emotionally hurt me, it worked. Something told me there was more to it.

The intruder—or whoever sent him to my apartment—wanted me to know that.

I was too exhausted and emotionally drained to think about it much longer. When Ian finally pulled into the driveway of our family home and let me out of the car, it was all I could do to follow him to the front door.

Rafe was with us—Rafe, who had also remained wordless in the car. It hadn't escaped me that Ian clearly worked out what had been going on, and I knew Rafe was going to be the one to pay for my stupidity. I was the one who'd wanted to run away. I had to ensure Ian was set straight...for both of our sakes.

I wished I hadn't fought the urge to leave Las Vegas without going to my apartment first—had we simply left, I'd never have known what happened. I wouldn't feel this ache in my chest knowing someone wanted to hurt me in the worst way possible. I could have remained wild and carefree with Rafe, living wherever we wanted and however we wanted.

It was a pipedream. It had always been a pipedream. I should have counted myself lucky I even got to experience fifteen minutes of it.

Rafe subtly squeezed my hand behind Ian's back before we entered the house, giving me a small, reassuring smile that didn't entirely reach his eyes. I didn't have it in me to smile back. I was empty.

When I saw my father in the hallway, I rushed to him and collapsed into his arms, sobbing profusely. I'd thought I couldn't possibly have any more tears to cry—how wrong I was.

"It's okay, it's all right," my dad murmured soothingly as he crushed me against him.

"Kirsten, you're okay," came a female voice—Katya, followed closely behind her by Patrick. I'd forgotten she was spending a few days getting to know her real father, but I was suddenly so very glad she was here.

I pulled away from my father. "I'm going to—I'm going up to bed. Katya, will you come with me?" I asked, my voice rough and hoarse from tears and disuse. Katya nodded her head, taking hold of my hand as I reached her side. "Rafe can —he can fill you in on what happened better than I can."

"I'll send the housekeeper up with some food," my father said, smiling warmly at me as I walked up the stairs.

"Thanks, Da." I glanced at Rafe one final time. I was sorry to put him in a position where he'd have to explain what happened without me, but I simply didn't have it in me either to tell everyone about it or listen to him recount it.

When I reached my childhood bedroom, I headed straight for the adjoining bathroom and removed my make-up. I looked a complete mess—my mascara was halfway down my face, marking the tracks my tears had taken. My skin was red and blotchy from the crying, too. It wasn't a pretty sight. Returning to my bedroom, I saw Katya rifling through a drawer. She glanced at me when she noticed my return.

"Just looking for some pajamas for us," she explained as she pulled out some oversized, soft cotton shirts. I took one from her, removing my hoodie but keeping my shorts on, throwing the shirt on before removing my bra; Katya went through a similar routine to get changed. I then collapsed on my king-sized bed just as Katya did the same.

"Do you want to talk about it?" she asked.

I turned my head to look at her. Katya's beautiful eyes were full of sadness and concern. She could tell it clearly wasn't merely a break-in I'd encountered.

"They took the only photo that exists of me with my mother, just after I was born and hours before she died."

Katya's eyes filled with tears as she hugged me. "I'm so sorry, Kirsten. I didn't know that. I had no photos of my mother until your dad gave me one. I know what your pain feels like."

I'd forgotten Yuri had erased all traces of her mother. "I don't talk about it much, because it's so painful," I murmured, rolling out of the hug to lie on my back. I stared at the ceiling.

"My dad pretty much raised me and my brothers all on his own. We all turned out okay, so I guess you could say he did a good job." I chuckled half-heartedly. "That's not really doing him justice—he's the best dad anyone could ask for."

"Then I should count myself 'lucky' he's my real dad, and not Yuri," Katya joked, making a shameless pun on my father's mob nickname.

"I take it the two of you have been getting to know each other?"

"Definitely. He's nothing like Yuri was—it's like he actually sees me as a person, rather than a commodity."

"That's because he does. He might be a mob boss, but he's my dad first, and he's never once seen me as anything other than a child he loves. He's never even brought up the subject of marriage, let alone a politically minded one, for me."

"You sure that's not because he thinks you're hopeless?"

I let out a bark of genuine laughter. "What a question. You might be right."

"Do you think it's because he knows you love Rafe?"

I paused for a second. "He doesn't want me involved with Rafe. Not because he doesn't want me to choose who I want, but because me being with Rafe has ramifications for the mob whether I want it to or not. I guess he just wants me to be with someone completely out of this life, so I can be, too."

"Christ, he really is the polar opposite of Yuri," Katya remarked. "Did I tell you he wanted me to marry Sergei?"

"*No!* Oh God, that would have been awful."

Katya shook her head slightly. "Awful in the sense that it

would have been romantically loveless, but Sergei himself isn't all that bad. He's reasonable, at least."

Suddenly, an idea struck. I rolled over onto my front and looked at Katya. "I don't suppose you could ask him if he's heard anything from the Russian side about the distribution of veterinary drugs on the streets? Or about anything to do with the break-in at my apartment?"

"I suppose I could. I'm not sure how much Sergei would actually tell me, given that I'm supposed to be out of the whole mob life, but it's worth a shot. I'll contact him tomorrow and see if I can get him to meet you."

Maybe after meeting with Sergei, I could finally make some headway and work out what was going on. It was worth a shot, at least.

"Thanks," I said, then jumped a little in surprise when the door to my bedroom clicked open.

It was our housekeeper, Clara, with a plate full of sandwiches.

"I'm sorry I couldn't prepare you anything warm, but your father insisted on getting food up to you as soon as possible," Clara apologized. "That bottle of vodka you used to hide in your wardrobe is still there, too, if you want something with a bit of a kick."

She grinned as I rolled my eyes.

"Of course you knew about that."

"I know about everything that goes on in this house, Miss O'Leary."

"I'll have you know it's Doctor O'Leary now."

Clara waved a hand dismissively as she made her way back to the door. "You'll always be the little miss to me, Kirsten. Try to get a good night's sleep, now."

"Thanks, Clara."

I hadn't thought I had much of an appetite, but after the first bite of a sandwich, I realized I was ravenous. Between the two of us, the platter was very quickly scarfed down, leaving nothing but crumbs within minutes.

"Ahh, I feel fat now," Katya remarked after patting her stomach. I scoffed at the comment.

"Hardly. I don't think I've ever seen someone with as good a figure as you in real life."

"I thought sisters were supposed to insult you incessantly, not give you compliments?"

"I think it's a bit of both."

"Well, then—your face looks awful right now, Kirsten. Does that balance us out?"

I gave her the finger. "I'm not sure that's how it works, but you can be damn sure the next time you're fishing for compliments, I'll flat out insult you."

Katya smiled. "I'll keep that in mind."

We lay in peaceful silence for a while, and I realized all at once I was actually drifting off to sleep. I knew I'd never have been able to sleep if I was by myself, which only made me appreciate Katya's presence all the more.

"Thanks for being here," I said quietly, the words almost lost in my massive bedroom.

"Any time." There was a pause, then Katya asked, "What

were you and Rafe doing, by the way? It was a bit late to have a meeting about your case."

I looked away, grimacing as I did so. "We'd been drinking and maybe planning on running away together…"

Katya sat up in shock. "No way! The two of you are like a full-on Romeo and Juliet. Are you still planning on it?"

"Given everything that happened tonight, I somehow doubt it," I breathed. "It wouldn't have been fair to anyone to have done it anyway. It was a silly, tipsy dream."

"Kirsten, that's so sad."

"I know."

"We'll find out who's behind all of this."

"I can only hope we do."

Katya hugged me once more, then moved off the bed to turn off the light.

"It's time the two of us got some sleep. Trust me—you'll need to be well-rested if you're going to face off against Sergei."

"You think I'll be able to meet him tomorrow?"

Katya laughed. "No, but you definitely need at least two nights worth of sleep before you're ready to talk to him."

"So mean."

"I'm your sister; I get to be mean."

"Something tells me I'm going to regret this relationship."

She turned off the light and returned to the bed. I could tell Katya was grinning even in the darkness.

"You're stuck with me whether you want me or not, big sister."

"Huh. I hadn't thought about the fact that you're younger than me."

"Guess that means you're not the 'little miss' anymore."

"You trying to usurp my position in the O'Leary household?"

Our banter continued in this way for another few minutes, the easy back-and-forth of it calm and relaxing. When I found myself drifting off, I didn't try to fight it. Katya was right. I needed the rest if I was going to work out who the hell was after me.

CHAPTER FOURTEEN

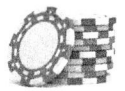

This was, quite potentially, the most awkward and intense discussion I'd ever been a part of. Not because I was the one who had to do most of the talking. I kept waiting for Liam O'Leary to ask why I'd been with Kirsten when we reached her apartment, but he never did. Neither did Ian tell his father for me. He didn't even give me any dirty looks.

Clearly, it was Ian's intention to keep his discovery of Kirsten and my botched runaway attempt between the two of us—for this, I was thankful. It was hardly as if we were going to try it again anyway...well, certainly not anytime soon.

Liam and Patrick had both reacted much as Ian had to the knowledge that Kirsten's only photo of herself as a baby with her mother had been stolen—shocked, but not in a 'why would they take that?' kind of way. They acted more in an 'I know who's likely behind this, and that isn't good' kind of way.

I decided to bite the bullet and ask, "Is there something significant about Kirsten's photo being taken?"

Ian glared at me. "It's not something you need to—"

"If I'm defending her as her lawyer, then yes, I need to know, Ian," I interrupted, predicting what he was going to say.

Liam raised a hand to prevent anyone else from speaking. "Though my son's tone was wrong, the matter truly is something you would previously never have needed to know, Rafe." He let out a frustrated breath. "Kirsten doesn't even know. And I don't want her to know, so what I'm about to tell you isn't to leave this room. Is that clear?"

Ian looked as if he was going to complain. I'd never kept anything from Kirsten in the past—back when we spent all our time together—so why would I start now?

"If it'll help me understand what's going on here and allow me to clear Kirsten's name, then I'll gladly keep this from her," I replied, keeping my eyes on Liam, willing him to see how serious I was.

Liam seemed satisfied by my answer, while Ian looked defeated, as if he were sure I would prove them wrong. Patrick, on the other hand, had barely said a word since I'd entered the O'Leary household. I'd always found it difficult to work out what the man was thinking, and right now was no exception. He did, however, stand up and walk over to a cabinet, returning with some whiskey and four glasses. It was the same kind Kirsten had brought over to my house. That felt like years ago but was, in reality, only a few hours ago.

I gladly accepted a glass. It was only after all four of us

had taken long drinks of the fiery, amber liquid that Liam began his explanation.

"When I married Jane—their mother," Liam began, gesturing at his sons, "there was one lad in particular who was very unhappy: Brian Feldman. He'd pined after Jane all throughout high school, but when she finally relented and went out with the guy in her senior year, he was a complete and utter psychopath. He wanted to know where she was at all times, who she was seeing, what she was eating—you get the picture. She tried to break it off several times, but Brian just wouldn't listen to her."

"Anyway," he continued, "Jane and I had known each other for years through our friends, though we'd never really spoken. But I'd noticed the way this guy was sneaking around, watching her, and I kind of…I don't know, took it upon myself to protect her. I guess a mob lifestyle has benefits in particular situations."

Liam chuckled at his own joke. I was painfully aware I was learning of how Liam and his late-wife had first got together—but the uncensored version. All Kirsten, and therefore I, knew was that Liam and Jane had been high school sweethearts who married straight after they graduated. I'd always known the real story couldn't have been as rose-tinted as Kirsten understood it to be.

"Once Jane realized what I was doing on her behalf, we got close very quickly. Brian didn't like that at all. He couldn't get near her when I was around. He assumed we were together, which infuriated him. He'd always hated that I belonged to a powerful family and he didn't. He never quit looking for an in. He went from syndicate to syndicate, trying to earn a position anywhere, but everyone saw him for the scumball he was.

"As for Jane and me…I guess we kept up the charade for so long, we ended up actually falling for each other."

I'd never seen Liam with such a happy, nostalgic look on his face. He clearly cherished the memory of how he and his wife fell in love.

He continued. "Brian didn't want to give up. Jane ended up having to get a restraining order against him when we graduated. She and I married pretty quickly after graduation—everyone assumed it was because she was pregnant, but we just…we knew we wanted to be together. Patrick wasn't born for another two years, so that quashed the shotgun wedding theory pretty quickly. Ian followed just over a year later. Brian hadn't bothered Jane since she'd filed the restraining order, so we assumed he'd finally moved on with his life. I couldn't imagine being happier than I was back then."

Then Liam's face darkened. "But I was wrong about Brian having moved on. One night, when Jane was returning from a night class—she had her sights set on studying vet medicine. Funny, because I've never told Kirsten that. Anyway, Brian cornered her. He demanded that she return to him, saying he'd never accepted their break-up, so, in his reality, the two of them were still together. And then—and then—"

Liam paused and downed his whiskey. I could tell what he

was going to say next. I'd sat in on enough sexual assault cases by now to know. Liam looked at my face.

"Well, clearly you've worked out what happened. Someone saw him before he could drag her away someplace else and called the police. Brian ran from the scene before they arrived. My poor Jane was a mess, as you would expect. A few of my guys found Brian a couple days later and beat him half to death. Lord knows I wanted him dead, but we handed him over to the police, and he was found guilty of his crimes. He went to jail for years. I never heard from or saw him again after he was released."

Everyone was silent as I took in this information. Clearly, this had all been kept under wraps. I was certain nobody in the Italian mob knew of what happened to the then-queen of the Irish mob.

"So how does Kirsten play into all of this?" I asked, not sure I really wanted to know anymore.

Liam growled. "Nine months after Brian attacked Jane, Kirsten was born."

"Oh shit."

He shook his head. "She's definitely mine," he quickly added. "You can tell just by looking at her that she's mine, but Jane insisted we had Kirsten's blood type tested, too. Even if she'd been Brian's, I'd have loved her like she was my own because she was Jane's too, but I can't tell you how relieved I ultimately was that she was truly my daughter."

"Did Brian know about the pregnancy?"

Liam frowned. "I'm sure he didn't know when he was in

prison, but like I said, nobody has seen nor heard from him since he was released. Considering what happened tonight, it's highly probable he does know."

"If Brian has cause to think Kirsten is his own daughter, why would he frame her for drug distribution?"

Liam rubbed his stubbly chin. "Possibly to get back at me for taking something he considered his—twice. But I don't know. I guess that's what we have to find out."

My head was swimming, drowning in everything I'd seen and heard over the past few hours. The whiskey probably didn't help with clarity. It was all so confusing.

"Don't you dare tell Kirsten," Ian threatened. "Make up some lie as to the leads you're following to have the court drop her case, just don't tell her the truth."

I looked at my best friend pointedly. "Ian, if you think I could tell Kirsten about anything I've just heard, then you really don't know me at all. No woman needs to know her mother was assaulted. This—I don't even know how I'm supposed to process all of this. But…I'm so sorry. For all of you. What happened to Jane was…beyond awful."

All three of the men in front of me had unreadable, stoic expressions plastered on their faces—I knew none of them was particularly great at dealing with sympathy and condolences.

"I couldn't save her mother, but I'll be damned if I won't save her." Liam knocked back his whiskey before staring at me. "Just get my daughter free of all this, then for the love of

God get her out of this forsaken city. I know she loves it, but it's not safe for her."

I felt my insides freeze. "You…knew? About—"

"Well, I know for sure, now that you've confirmed it," Liam said with a humorless laugh. "I've had an inkling for a long time now the two of you would end up together. It's not as if Kirsten has ever been interested in anyone else. You seem to have actually done a pretty grand job of staying out of the mob, so lately I've been running out of reasons to disapprove of you, Rafe Wilde."

I didn't know how to take that. The approval of Kirsten's father made me happy, but Liam didn't know what I'd done to ensure Sergei sailed smoothly to the top of the Russian mob. I wouldn't count that as staying out of the life he didn't want for his daughter, but I could hardly admit to it out loud.

Instead, I smiled slightly and then checked the time. "I should really be heading back home before it gets too late."

Ian glanced at me. "I'll drive you."

His father shook his head. "Don't be ridiculous. Rafe can stay here tonight. Clara has already prepared the guest bedroom on the first floor for you. I don't know what might have happened if you weren't with my daughter tonight…and I don't want to dwell on it. So please stay the night. It's the least I can do to say thank you."

God, Liam really was a good man, and a great father. Not for the first time, I wondered why he was the head of the Irish mob in the first place.

Patrick stood up from the table. "I'll show you where the

room is," he said. I was surprised—it's not as if Patrick and I had ever talked much.

I followed him after saying, "Thank you for the hospitality, Mr. O'Leary. Rest assured, I will clear Kirsten's name. You can be damn certain of that." I glanced at Ian. "I'll speak to you in the morning."

Ian said nothing, but he didn't seem nearly as livid as he'd been earlier. Maybe having his father approve of me being with Kirsten was enough to suppress his overprotective nature. I could only hope.

When Patrick showed me to the guest bedroom, he turned to me and said, "I'll talk to Ian. He's gotten out of hand lately, especially towards you. I don't know what's gotten into him."

I smiled in gratitude. "Thanks, Patrick."

"And for what it's worth, I was always hoping the two of you would end up together. You were about the only person who could convince Kirsten not to always do the first stupid thing that popped into her head."

I laughed. "I'm fairly certain she still managed to rope me into doing those stupid things more often than I managed to talk her out of them."

"Then I shudder to think what she could have gotten into without you around!"

Patrick left me in the corridor. I recognized the door to Kirsten's old room sitting ajar just down the hallway, and out of curiosity, I walked over to it. Peeking through the open space, I saw Kirsten and Katya lying on the bed, huddled against each other as if they'd known each other their entire lives.

It was adorable and reassuring. I'd been worried Kirsten wouldn't be able to sleep at all tonight.

As I made my way back to the guest bedroom, I mulled over everything I'd been told tonight by Liam O'Leary. I had to wonder, how was I supposed to sleep tonight?

CHAPTER FIFTEEN

I'd almost forgotten how good a decent night of sleep could be. Though I knew my life was likely going to get a lot worse before it got better, I felt refreshed. After all, I'd been charged with a dangerous crime I hadn't committed. I couldn't leave the city. I couldn't work. Someone who may be involved in the crime I was framed for had broken into my apartment. They took away the only physical evidence I was my mother's one and only daughter…

Then my attempt to run away with the man I loved had been botched. One could say there were no circumstances under which I could feel better today, and yet I did. Maybe it was the excessive crying, or maybe it was the fact that I knew Rafe reciprocated my feelings. Maybe it was because Katya and I had talked well into the night until we both fell into an exhausted sleep. Maybe it was all of them. Whatever the cause, I felt like I could tackle anything thrown my way today, which could only be a good thing.

Katya wasn't lying beside me when I woke up. The sound of running water from my bathroom told me where my half-sister was. Wondering what time it was, I picked up my cell phone from the bedside table, only to discover it had no charge left.

"Katya, do you have a phone charger?" I called out, loudly enough that she could hear me above the water.

"In my bag," she managed to gurgle out. Clearly, she was brushing her teeth. Chuckling at the noise she made, I walked over to her bag and got her charger, impatiently waiting for my phone to turn back on once I plugged it in. When the time flashed on the screen, I clucked my tongue in annoyance. It was well past noon.

I had wasted so much of the day already, but I'd needed the sleep.

When Katya vacated the bathroom, I went in and freshened up, then signaled for Katya to join me for breakfast in the kitchen.

"Surely, we're getting lunch, considering the time," she said wryly as we made our way down the stairs.

"Ah, but technically the first thing you eat in a day, regardless of the time, is breakfast. You're breaking your fast and all that."

She rolled her eyes. "Of course you're a 'technically' person. At least you seem to be doing better."

"Much better, all things considered."

The kitchen was an odd sight to behold, to say the least. My father and two brothers sat at the kitchen table with Rafe, who to my surprise didn't look nearly as awkward as I would have expected.

"I didn't realize you stayed the night, Rafe," I said as we locked eyes. He smiled slightly.

"I couldn't pass up your father's hospitality, especially given how late it was."

Ah, so they'd stayed up late, too. Eyeing the four men at the table, I noticed all of them looked somewhat haggard and sleep-deprived. Something told me alcohol had been involved.

When Katya and I sat down, Clara brought over a fresh pile of pancakes. My eyes lit up when I saw them.

"Clara, you're an angel."

"Don't get used to it, or you'll gain too much weight."

"You wound me," I replied with mock hurt as I eagerly piled my plate with soft, fluffy pancakes loaded with maple syrup.

"You seem much better this morning," Ian commented.

I could tell there was some lingering tension between my brother and Rafe, though my elder brother Patrick and my father seemed completely unperturbed by it.

"Turns out sleep does wonders. Who'd have known?"

"Certainly not a sleep-deprived vet, that's for sure," my sister said.

"Katya, could you pass me the syrup?" I responded.

Breakfast passed in this way for a while—easy, pleasant and without so much as one serious question. When my father coughed slightly, making it obvious he was going to announce something, we all froze.

He laughed at the silence. "Why so serious? I have a request—a humble one, in my opinion, that I hope you'll be happy to oblige."

Oh, that got us all curious. Katya quirked an eyebrow.

"Do you always speak so mysteriously, Liam?" she asked. Katya had told me the evening before she was still unsure as to how she should address my father. 'Dad' was far too forward considering the short amount of time they'd spent together, whereas 'Mr. O'Leary' seemed too formal.

There was a glint in his eye as he replied, "Only when I want to ensure folk are listening."

My brothers and I collectively rolled our eyes. Rafe and Katya looked confused.

"He does this all the time to 'impress' people," Patrick explained. He looked pointedly at our father. "Just spill it, Dad. Some of us actually have work to do this afternoon."

Liam laughed. "All I'm asking is for all of you to join me for dinner tomorrow evening. That means you too, Rafe, and Katya—can you bring Matt? I'd like to get to know my son-in-law a little better."

Now the stunned silence was appropriate. An O'Leary, Wilde, and Petrenko dinner? Nothing of the sort had ever been heard of before.

My father would be the one who wanted to organize one. Something was telling me there was more to this dinner than met the eye, but I knew better than to question his motives in front of everyone. That would get me nowhere—I'd have to use my own wits to work it out.

Rafe glanced at me, though I had no idea what the look meant. "I'd be happy to, Liam," he eventually said. "I know for a fact Matt is free, so don't let him try to weasel out, Katya."

She laughed. "Good to know. I look forward to it."

Ian looked like he wanted to protest, but Patrick gave him a scathing look that kept him quiet. It wasn't often Patrick put his foot down, but whenever he did, it was a stark reminder that he would one day take over for our father as the head of the Irish mob—and he was perfect for it. Everybody listened to him when he had something to say, even Ian. I was so glad he was here.

Rafe stood up and shook my father's hand. "I'd best be off, Liam. I told the firm I was working on a case outside of the office this morning—which isn't untrue—but I really need to get back to work."

Liam smiled. "Of course, Rafe. I'll see you tomorrow evening."

Rafe had only just vacated the kitchen when I pushed away from the table and rushed after him. I grabbed onto his sleeve just as he reached the front door.

"You okay?" I asked.

His eyes widened. "Why are you asking me that? After what happened last night, the only person who should be checked in on is you."

"Someone breaking into my apartment doesn't change the

fact that we were going to run away together. That it failed. I'm kind of—I don't know—confused. Where does that put us now?"

Rafe pulled me in for a hug. "It puts us in a terrible position, which we nonetheless have to deal with. Your case just got far more serious, so we both need to concentrate on that, okay? Running off might have solved some of our problems, but to solve them all, we need to stay."

"I know…" I mumbled into his shirt. My chest tightened and constricted. Life wasn't fair. Why was our timing always so off?

He lifted my head up with a finger curled underneath my chin. "I'll see you tomorrow. Don't you dare go back to your apartment. I'll swing by and grab some of your things and bring them with me. You can hold out until then, I take it?"

I sighed dramatically. "I guess so. I wasn't going to go back anyway. I'm not an idiot. And I—I slept better here than I had in my own apartment for a long time. I think staying here is what I need to do right now."

Rafe smiled. "Good. Well, I really better—"

"Oh wait," I said, suddenly remembering my conversation with Katya from the night before. "I'm going to meet Sergei in a couple days to see if he's heard anything about my case from the Russian mob side."

Rafe frowned. "Is that a good idea? I should come with you."

"No, I think it'll work out better if it's just me and Katya. I'll fill you in after the meeting, okay?"

Rafe ran a hand through his hair, looking tired and resigned. "You have to tell me everything. You can't just cherry-pick, got that? I know what you can be like when obscuring the truth."

"Says the lawyer."

That drew a chuckle from Rafe. "Touché. I'll see you tomorrow," he said, kissing me on the cheek before leaving the house.

It felt like we'd taken three massive strides forward yesterday, only to take a race car back today. I knew all I had to do was be patient. We were going to work out who was behind my frame-job and the break-in, and then Rafe and I could finally be together. Or, at the very least, work out what we were to each other. That felt like a lifetime away.

In the meantime, I had a dinner to prepare for. With my clothes all locked up in my apartment, I had nothing to wear. That meant shopping, something I hadn't done in a long, long time.

Grinning despite myself, I re-entered the kitchen and asked, "Katya, do you feel like looking at dresses this afternoon?"

Katya's smile was luminous.

"Absolutely."

CHAPTER SIXTEEN

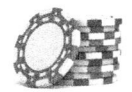

I didn't think I'd ever been this nervous for a dinner, which was saying something, considering I'd grown up surrounded by the Italian mob.

Everyone had dressed for the occasion, especially Kirsten and Katya, who were wearing stunning dresses in copper and silver, respectively. They looked like otherworldly goddesses.

"I don't know how girls manage to do it," Ian muttered as we mingled with glasses of champagne in hand. Liam had booked a small, private dining room in his favorite Italian restaurant—clearly a nod to Matt and me. Something we both readily appreciated for the gesture it was. We waited for the man in question to arrive before we sat down. Patrick arrived with his father. Surely, he'd been busy with the O'Leary family accounts all day. I wasn't the only man who didn't stop working on the weekend.

"No, but seriously," Ian continued. "How is it that you two were slumming in ponytails and pajamas while eating pancakes yesterday, and now you and Kirsten look like bloody angels?"

Kirsten punched him on the arm. "You're such a charmer."

"My wife is always gorgeous, especially in a ponytail and pajamas," Matt said, sliding an arm around Katya's waist as he kissed her on the cheek. She blushed beautifully as she smiled.

"You don't scrub up too badly yourself, Matt," she replied, turning to fix his tie slightly.

"It must be a Wilde brother thing," Kirsten added as she helped herself to another glass of champagne, sending a sly grin my way. "Alex dresses pretty sharply, too. Wonder how long it'll take before Dad invites him for family dinners so he doesn't feel left out."

"Now, now, better not to start wishing for the impossible," Ian joked.

Liam and Patrick made their way through the dining area to the sounds of the five of us laughing at Ian's joke.

"Good to see everyone in good spirits already," Liam announced as I handed him a glass of champagne, after which he took a seat. I handed another glass to Patrick, who took it from me with a tired smile on his face. He looked pretty exhausted, as if he needed around three days worth of sleep.

"Long day?" I asked him sympathetically.

"No different from any other. I need a vacation." Patrick and Ian sat. Matt held a chair out for Katya, so I followed suit for Kirsten. It made me wonder, was this a test dinner to see if

I could suitably date Liam O'Leary's daughter? It was a concept that made me nervous, so I tried not to think about it.

"You look stunning," I murmured into Kirsten's ear as she sat down. I was happy to see her skin flush.

When Matt and I sat, Liam raised his glass, so we all followed suit.

"I never imagined I would have two of the Wilde brothers sitting down to dinner with my family, let alone a Petrenko, even if said Petrenko is really an O'Leary." He smiled warmly for Katya. "This can only mean good things for our families if we work together. So, here's to working together."

Liam almost imperceptibly looked at me as everyone clinked their glasses, so did Patrick and Ian. It wasn't difficult to know what those looks meant.

You're working with us now, like it or not. You know our family secrets, so you better step up to the challenge and not fail us.

I barely suppressed a gulp. Now I was definitely nervous, especially when Kirsten smiled at me curiously. It wouldn't take long for her to realize I was hiding something. She was far too sharp to miss even a small change in my behavior. Even if she was gloriously oblivious to male attention, she was never oblivious to me.

I briefly thought of Dean Collins and about how Kirsten was going to let the man down. Gently, but firmly, I hoped. Despite everything, I knew deep down he was a decent man who clearly cared for her on more than just a romantic level.

But that's a trivial matter for now, I thought as the first round of dishes were brought over to the table on large, silver platters.

"So, Rafe," Liam began, between mouthfuls of ravioli, "you played basketball in college, didn't you? Do you still play?"

"Not anymore, unfortunately. My days of playing the sport are long gone."

"Replaced with drinking sessions and takeout Chinese food dates with yours truly," Ian announced.

"I swear, Ian, if you were the one who wanted to date Rafe instead of Kirsten, you'd have absolutely no issue with the matter," Patrick quipped easily.

Kirsten literally spat her champagne out at the comment, she laughed so hard.

"That's so damn true. Oh my God, why did I not see—"

"Language at the table, love," Liam chided.

"As if you care about language at our usual family dinners, Dad."

"Ahh, but as you can see, we have guests."

"Who are practically family. May as well let them see us at our worst, or maybe our best."

Liam let out an exaggerated sigh. "I can't think who you possibly take after with this behavior in the slightest."

Patrick and Ian exchanged a knowing glance but didn't say anything. It made me wonder if Kirsten took after her mother in personality as well as her looks—though she had her father's eyes. I was told her mother's eyes had been the palest blue a person could imagine. It was something Ian had once told me in a drunken stupor one night. It was the only thing he professed to remember about the woman—her eyes.

I found that unbelievably sad. Was it worse for someone to forget all but one detail of a person they loved or have no memories of the person in the first place?

I shook my head slightly. It wasn't a subject to be thought about in the middle of dinner with the O'Learys.

"How's the casino running, Matt?" Patrick asked my brother politely.

"Much better now that the Russians don't have their hands in the vault anymore," he replied, smiling at Katya.

"Rafe had something to do with that somehow, didn't he?"

I stared at Patrick, shocked. How could he possibly know? I hadn't told anyone.

Matt winced slightly. "That's not common knowledge, Patrick. How did you—"

"Just a hunch. Thanks for confirming it."

"Bloody bastard, Patrick," Kirsten cussed, earning her a stern look from her father.

Patrick laughed. "It's not as if I'll tell anyone. If anything, I'm impressed by the fact you all got away with whatever it was you did in the first place."

Clearly, we'd all been underestimating Patrick for far too long. He was going to make a formidable mob boss when he took over for his father. Not for the first time, I was grateful my brothers and I were out of the game.

Well, almost out of the game in my case. As much as I hated for Katya to pull some strings to have a meeting with

Sergei, I understood why it was necessary. Had Kirsten not already arranged the meeting, I would have tried to broker one myself.

Kirsten was right. It was better to leave the Sergei stuff to her and Katya. Clearly, Sergei and Katya had some innate understanding going on. I had no doubt she'd be able to wrangle the information we needed out of him.

If that didn't help clear things up, then...

We were back to square one. Suddenly, I remembered I was supposed to have talked to Detective Peters yesterday. Maybe he had leads I could investigate. I had avoided the man's calls because I'd been busy processing everything Liam O'Leary had explained about his wife's past.

To be honest, I *still* didn't know how to treat it. As I watched Kirsten happily cuss and insult her brothers as she passed Katya and Matt the garlic bread, I understood why the men in Kirsten's family didn't want her to know anything. That meant I had to get better at hiding things from her.

"Something on your mind, Rafe?" Liam asked mildly.

"Just Kirsten," I let out before I could filter my thoughts, much to my horror. I clapped a hand over my mouth as she blushed furiously. Ian began to grow red for an entirely different reason. "I mean—"

Liam laughed uproariously, cutting off my feeble attempt at an excuse. "At least you're honest about it. I can't be having someone trying to court my daughter if he can lie to my face."

Lie to Kirsten, but don't lie to me, was what Liam was

getting at. Certainly, the man could tell what I had truly been thinking about in relation to his daughter.

I decided to stick to the truth as I responded, "I would never lie to you, Liam. I never have. Even when Kirsten and I were stealing your whiskey as teenagers, I never lied to you."

"Because you let her steal it so you couldn't be held accountable," Ian muttered. Despite his tone, there was a smirk on his face.

I waved the comment off. "Surely, you must realize by now I've only ever had Kirsten's best interests at heart. Now more than ever. I'd do anything for her. I hope you understand that."

There. I'd said it. It was possibly too serious a statement to have come out of my mouth midway through dinner, but what better time to announce my feelings than in front of the entire, extended O'Leary family?

Even Matt looked embarrassed for me.

And Kirsten...

She looked delightfully horrified. It caused me to grin foolishly in response.

"I suppose there may have been a better time or place to say that, but...I'm going to clear her name. When I do, I hope nobody will have reason to suggest Kirsten and I should not be together." I looked at Ian when I said that, but he looked away.

Obviously, Liam had suggested something along those lines the other night, but I had to be sure. I had to know, in no uncertain terms, that nothing was going to stand in our way once the charges were dropped against her.

Liam smiled, seemingly satisfied. "I couldn't have said it better myself. And you're no boy now, Rafe—you're a man. I'd have answered differently if you had come to me at eighteen saying something similar. Although, I know you'd been thinking the same back then."

"Patrick again?" Kirsten exclaimed, seeing the look on her oldest brother's face. "You were the only one who knew anything close to a confession was gonna happen."

I was confused. "Patrick, how…?"

"I overheard you and Rafe discussing it back in the day. I may have told my old man, and Ian may have heard us—"

"Ah, which is why he was so pissy with me before we started college. Now I get it."

"That and my girlfriend at the time broke up with me because she was in love with you, or did you forget that bit?" Ian threw out as he drank more champagne.

"Now that you mention it," Matt said, "I do seem to recall you having to push off a particularly persistent girl back then, Rafe…"

The evening descended into more and more raucous retellings of stories from our past much to Katya's delight. Despite the underlying seriousness of everything going on with Kirsten's case, and with the tale of her mother's ruin still playing in my ears, the evening brought with it promise.

This could be what our life could permanently be like after I cleared her name. It really could. Even Ian seemed to accept us begrudgingly, though he still didn't like it.

Underneath the table, I squeezed Kirsten's knee, then

found her hand and intertwined her fingers with mine. She glanced up at me from underneath her gorgeous, dark lashes as my fingers tightened around hers.

If this was what life with Kirsten O'Leary would be like, then I could certainly get used to it.

CHAPTER SEVENTEEN

Sergei was—scary. There was no doubt he ruled with an iron fist, and yet Katya seemed to be able to handle him like he was an overly large puppy. She'd mentioned to me before that, at first, she hadn't known how to deal with him either, but they'd eventually come to understand each other.

I had to wonder, how on *Earth* did she manage it?

Regardless, here the two of us were, drinking vodka with the head of the Russian mob, who rumor had it murdered Katya's 'father'. Katya didn't seem perturbed by this at all, even if it were true.

I suppose, given who her supposed father had turned out to be, I couldn't be surprised.

"So someone's out to get you, Miss Irish?" Sergei drawled, leaning back in his seat and drinking his vodka like he owned the place. Well, I guess he did—the bar we were sitting in was in Russian mob territory, after all.

"Possibly. Or," I said, taking a sip of vodka, "they're trying to incite political unrest between the mob factions. Maybe someone doesn't like that their Russian princess has turned out to be the daughter of a leprechaun and has since seceded the mob throne to give it to an outsider…namely you."

Sergei was silent for a moment, but then a grin slowly split open his face. He looked at Katya, then me. "I like your sister. She gets to the point so quickly."

Katya returned the smile. "I'm glad you approve."

And so was I, quite frankly. Sergei seemed to warm somewhat to me after that—though given how little I knew of the man, it could well have been a front.

"So have you heard or seen anything that might help the investigation out?" I asked, trying hard not to sound desperate, even though I was. I wanted my freedom back, and I wanted it yesterday. Without freedom, I could never have Rafe.

Sergei looked up at the ceiling in thought as he drank more vodka.

"Possibly…"

"That means yes, of course," Katya said plainly. "What do you know, Sergei? You know this whole mess will affect you as much as it affects Kirsten if it has anything to do with the Russian mob."

Sergei's eyes hardened. "I am aware of this, Katya. Have

you changed your mind about running the Russian mob and believe you would do a better job?"

"I get it. Explain at your own pace."

I couldn't believe Katya had the guts to speak to a man as imposing and intimidating as Sergei the way she did. Even with her credentials as the previous heir to his throne, she was being bold.

Sergei leaned in towards the table, lowering his voice until it was so quiet the two of us had to lean in, too.

"There's a faction that doesn't want me at the top. They could only accept me as the successor when I was marrying into the family through Katya, but now that that isn't happening," he stared pointedly at Katya, who returned the stare wholeheartedly, "I need to find a way to deal with them. They aren't massive, but they're big enough to warrant looking out for. They may be responsible—at least in part—for all of this drug distribution on Irish territory."

"How would that affect you, though? Other than the Irish going against the lot of you for believing it to be a frame job?"

Sergei's grin turned wicked. "That's exactly how it will affect me. Either they want me to buckle under the pressure, die trying, or they can use the chaos as a cover to take me out, then blame it on the Irish. You should really watch yourself, vet girl. They might even try to take you hostage to use as leverage."

Ah, damn. Just what I wanted to hear. Another reason for Rafe and my father and brothers to lock me up at home. Great.

"I don't suppose you know if any of these people are or

were related to my mother—Jane O'Leary, though her maiden name was Russell, I think?"

"Hell if I know. I'll keep an ear out for the name. Now that you've mentioned it, it's possible it has come up and I didn't know or care if it was important."

So far, the narrative seemed to be that the drug set-up was very much mob related, as I'd suspected it to be. So, was the break-in an entirely separate matter? In which case, who was behind that?

I could only hope the two were related, because it would make things easier to solve. Two birds with one stone and all that.

"Thanks, Sergei. Your information was really helpful."

"I'll keep you updated through Katya from now on," he replied, inclining his head before downing the rest of his vodka in one go. "It wouldn't look good for me to be meeting with you more than once in a short space of time."

He waved over his bodyguard, who handed him his coat.

"I'll be in touch, my lost love," he said to Katya, a wry smile on his face that caused my sister to roll her eyes.

"Hilarious. Thanks, Sergei."

And with that, the man and his bodyguard were gone, leaving Katya and me inside a Russian-owned bar in an area of Vegas I definitely didn't like.

Katya nearly jumped out of her skin when she looked at the time. "Oh shit. I'm late for Capone's. Sorry, Kirsten, but it's in the complete opposite direction from the vet clinic—that's where you're headed now, yeah?"

I waved a hand dismissively. "Don't worry about it. That's what online maps are for. If I get lost, I'll get a taxi." With a hug and a kiss goodbye, the two of us parted ways, leaving me to walk down a plethora of unknown, neon-adorned streets as I shifted between checking my path on my phone and keeping my eyes on the streets.

I had to admit, I didn't like walking about alone in Russian territory. Even with my status as the mob doctor, all it would take was one misstep, and I might find myself in trouble. That wasn't even taking into account what Sergei had said.

Someone may try to kidnap me.

It was the paranoia creeping up on me that made me feel as if I was being watched and followed. There was no way I actually was being followed. That was ridiculous. Nobody even knew I was here in the first place, save for Rafe—that had been the whole point.

I nearly jumped out of my skin when my phone buzzed in my hand. It was Dean.

"H-hello?" I let out, hating that it sounded like a nervous question.

"Hey, O'Leary. Are you okay? You sound a bit jumpy."

"I'm fine, I'm fine. Your call just gave me a fright."

"You can perform life-saving surgery on a Rottweiler, and yet a phone call has you scared?"

"Ha ha. Very funny. I'm heading over to the clinic now. I need to talk to you and Rose."

I could tell Dean didn't like the idea. "Kirsten, you know you can't come near the clinic, remember? I'm almost on lunch—I could meet you somewhere? I won't have long though."

I was ashamed to say I'd actually forgotten I wasn't allowed in or around the place. Bitterly, I suppressed a sigh. "That's okay, you don't have to do that. Just…keep an eye out for each other. Someone may try to harm you."

He immediately sounded concerned. "You have a genuine reason to believe that?"

"No—not yet. Nothing concrete, anyway. Just be careful, please? This whole drug charge may be much bigger than we anticipated, and I couldn't bear the idea of you or Rose getting caught in the crossfire."

"You gonna be my knight in shining armor, O'Leary?"

"Ugh, if I have to."

He laughed, which immediately put me at ease. "Let me take you out for dinner next Saturday. I can see if Rose is free, too. I think it would do you good to have something to look forward to…to take your mind off things. No doubt you'll have tons to vent about in a week's time."

I smiled, though he couldn't see it. "That sounds wonderful, Dean. Okay, I better get going and let you actually eat something for lunch."

"I can stay on the phone for a bit longer if you wanted to talk."

"I'm not that lonely. Even I have standards sometimes."

"Such a cruel woman. Okay, I'll leave you to it. Just know I'm only a phone call away if you change your mind. I'll see you on Saturday."

"Yep, see you then. Bye, Dean."

"Bye, O'Leary."

And with that, I was left to continue my solitary walk down streets I didn't recognize. My thoughts were the only things I had to keep me company.

Dean hadn't pushed for an answer in either direction as to whether I'd try going out with him. He had kept to his word—he was going to wait until my name was cleared. Even with that hanging over us, he still made sure I was okay and had someone to talk to. I felt an overwhelming sense of guilt that I'd been so willing to give up the life I'd built for myself at the Collins Vet Clinic with Dean and Rose and even Grace, the scatterbrained receptionist who was politely disinterested in any of our personal lives.

Did I really love Rafe so much that I could knowingly give it all up? If given the opportunity to make the decision again—sober this time—could I? Rafe had finally made his feelings clear to me and my family. Once I was exonerated, we could get the hell out of Vegas (legally this time). We'd finally be free of the city that was trying to consume us.

Even with everything going on, did I really want to leave? Yes, I loved Rafe. I loved him with all my heart, and I knew he wanted to get out of Vegas—it was the best move for his career, but was it the best move for me?

Was I ready to give up what few friends I had, a job I loved, and a blossoming relationship with a sister I never knew? It was a lot to throw away. I didn't even think I could easily give up my role as the mob doctor, now that I was considering it.

As I turned on to a street that was finally—thank God—familiar, I breathed a heavy sigh of relief. I couldn't make these decisions on my own. I had to discuss my future with the man I wanted to share it with—Rafe. He'd been clear that the case had to take priority for now. It was what everyone was clear on. I knew they were right.

That didn't make it any easier on me as the subject of the case. I wasn't living a life right now. I was under careful watch by the police and the detective on my case.

I shivered. *I don't feel like they're the* only *ones watching me.*

Even now, treading on familiar pavement and looking at recognizable neon lights, I still couldn't shake the feeling that there was a pair of eyes watching my every move. It made me feel unsafe. It made me feel vulnerable.

Taking the advice that I'd said I'd follow to Katya, I hailed a cab as soon as I could see one, asking the driver to take me home.

Suddenly I felt tired, but not in the way a double shift at the clinic always made me feel. So much for that positive energy I'd been filled with on Friday. It was only Sunday, and already I was drained.

One thing was for sure, I couldn't wait to have my life back, fourteen-hour shifts and all.

CHAPTER EIGHTEEN

"You know, when I said I wanted to talk with you tomorrow, Mr. Wilde, I really meant tomorrow. As in, the day after Dr. O'Leary's apartment had been broken into—not four days later."

"I assumed you wouldn't want to be disturbed on a weekend."

"You and I both know that's bullshit. You didn't return my calls. What did you find out that was so important you felt like you could ignore the lead detective on the case you're working on?"

I cracked my neck to release the tension. Detective Peters was right, I'd ignored him because I didn't know what to do. Things had gotten out of hand. Though I'd sworn never to tell Kirsten about what happened to her mother, I ultimately knew if I was going to clear her name, I had to divulge the case to Peters.

"Detective Peters—"

"Just call me Charles, Mr. Wilde."

"Then call me Rafe, and we can skip the formalities altogether."

Charles smiled somewhat dryly as he took a sip of his coffee. We were sitting in an unassuming café, which served subpar food but excellent coffee.

"Rafe it is, then. So, out with it. What have you found out?"

"Are you familiar with a sexual assault case against Jane O'Leary about twenty-seven years ago? You're a little young to have been on the force at the time, but I suppose it's possible."

Charles laughed humorlessly. "As it happens, I do vaguely recall a shockingly violent assault case that was closing up when I started as a rookie police officer. I believe that may have been the one. Is Jane O'Leary—"

"Kirsten's mother, yes. And no, the attacker isn't her father, just to set the record straight from the get-go."

"I take it that piece of information is relevant?"

"Possibly. The animal who was after her—Brian Feldman —was incarcerated before Jane knew she was pregnant. It's possible he heard on the prison grapevine she was, but whether he knew the fact that the baby wasn't his is yet to be seen. Nobody knows where Feldman is now or where he went after he was released. Liam O'Leary believes he may have played a part in the drug frame-job against Kirsten, since the only thing that was stolen from her apartment was the only photo that exists of Kirsten with her mother."

Charles was silent for a moment. "The break-in and the drug charges could be unrelated incidents. So while it sounds reasonable to suspect Feldman of being involved with the break-in, it's a bit of a stretch to say he's involved with the drugs."

"That may be so, but the simplest answer is usually the correct one, or so they say. It's a bit coincidental for two unrelated, serious incidents to happen to the same person in quick succession."

"But not impossible."

I resisted the urge to growl. I knew Charles was merely doing his job. "Kirsten had nothing to do with distributing those drugs. Surely, your investigation hasn't found any evidence against her other than what was planted? I bet those 'witnesses' have all but disappeared."

"I'm not at liberty to discuss that," Charles replied, but I could see through the steely façade he'd put on—even he knew Kirsten was innocent.

"The drug thing is clearly mob related, no doubt about it," I continued, "which I imagine will be huge for you if you manage to find the guys responsible for the frame-job. How Kirsten herself relates to all of it could merely be because of who her father is, or as a means to an end, or it could be personal. I've investigated the personal argument to its death —there's nobody who wishes harm against Kirsten O'Leary simply for being Kirsten O'Leary."

"I reached that conclusion, too."

"So that leaves us with an attack against her father, or a means to an end."

Charles smiled wryly. "Us?"

"Look, I don't care if you're not at liberty to discuss what you've found out so far, but in all honesty—I can tell you have jack squat. Kirsten is caught in the crossfire of something bigger than herself, and that's not something I want escalating. I was fine with merely getting her name cleared at first, but now…now, I fear if the perpetrators themselves aren't found and taken out, she'll remain in danger even after she's found innocent. That's not something I'm willing to accept. So let me work with you."

"Is this where you tell me you have useful contacts and information I'd never be privy to by virtue of me being a police detective and you being a Wilde?"

I smiled slightly. "If that works, then yes."

Charles grinned. "I'll admit, we're at a standstill right now. If we could keep up an information exchange, that might bring some things to light we weren't aware of individually."

"Thank you, Charles. I don't suppose you could look into the Feldman case file to see if he has a last known address?"

"Already on it," Charles replied, pulling out his cell phone to send a message. He glanced up at me. "Are you already privy to information I'm likely unaware of?"

"I will be in a couple hours. Kirsten met up with Sergei Volkov, with Katya Petrenko acting as an intermediary. I think he had some information from the Russian side that will prove valuable."

"Update me on that as soon as you hear back from them, and I'll forward on any relevant information about Feldman to you. And Rafe—"

"Yes?"

"This is in your capacity as a lawyer, so I fully expect you not to divulge any of this information to persons not investigating this case. That includes your family and the O'Leary family. Especially Dr. O'Leary."

"That's a given."

Charles checked the time on his watch, then swigged down the last of his coffee. "I best be off, then. Contact me about the Volkov meeting when you can."

"Got it. Thanks, Charles."

"Rafe."

I was left sitting by myself, mulling over the choices I made as I stared sightlessly into the dregs of my Americano.

I felt awful keeping things from Kirsten—especially everything related to her mother, but the gravity of the situation she was in, as well as how painful the story of what happened to Jane O'Leary was, meant I knew I couldn't tell her a thing. As a lawyer, that was obvious.

As her…I didn't know what we were. More than friends. More than a fling—hell, we hadn't even slept together yet. We were less than a couple…at least for now. As her 'something', it was tearing me apart to be lying to her. She didn't deserve it.

"She doesn't deserve *anything* that's happened to her lately," I muttered aloud, drawing curious looks from the people in the next booth over. I didn't care. They could look all they wanted. I needed to figure everything out, but there were vital pieces of information missing.

With any luck, Detective Peters would be able to track down Feldman's last known location, and if we were even luckier, speak to some men who were in prison with him. Kirsten's meeting with Sergei could have brought many things to light. I could only hope.

I pushed away my coffee cup, stood up and visited the restroom before leaving. I stared at myself in the mirror—God, the lack of sleep and stress from the case were giving me black eyes.

Was this my life now? Was every stressful case I worked on going to chip away at my exterior until I looked twenty years older than I actually was? It was easy to deal with all of this for Kirsten's sake, but what about later?

Was I really cut out for law as a career? It wasn't something I'd considered before. I hadn't really had a choice. My father had told me I'd go into law. In truth, I'd reveled in the challenge and competition of studying it at college—trying to best my peers (especially Ian). I got a high from cracking a particularly difficult case, getting the top grade in all of my classes. It had all been one big game.

It seemed like a stupidly obvious thing to say, but it definitely didn't feel like a game now. I doubted I'd ever get that feeling back. If the rest of my career was going to be like this case—slowly draining the life out of me while making me wonder whether there was that much difference between being a member of the mob and legally defending crooked clients—did I want it? Was this really what I wanted for myself?

I shook my head, watching the motion in the mirror as I did so. Now was not the time for such thoughts. I could think about myself later.

After all, Kirsten had wanted to leave Vegas. There was no reason why we couldn't do that after we had whoever framed her behind bars. We could go anywhere. I wouldn't even have to be a lawyer. The idea sounded alluring.

So hold on to it, Rafe, I told myself. *Hold on to that dream and get through the next few weeks. Just hold on.*

It was all well and good to tell myself this, another experience to live through the next few weeks, but I had to do it for Kirsten. I had to. The look on her face as she kneeled on the floor of her bedroom staring at a broken and empty picture frame was more than I could bear. I never wanted to see that look on her face again.

Determination renewed, I blasted my face with cold water from the sink, dried off with a handful of scratchy paper towels, then left the restroom and café altogether.

I could do this. Just a few more weeks, and Kirsten and I could leave. We even had her family's blessing—well, as much as I could have ever hoped for.

I just had to get through the next few weeks.

CHAPTER NINETEEN

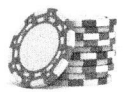

Five days later, and I still couldn't shake the fact that it felt like I was being followed. I didn't understand the feeling. I barely left my father's house, let alone go anywhere remotely sketchy, even if I'd wanted to, but I didn't.

I just wanted to be safe, even if that meant staying holed up at home most of the time. I hadn't told Rafe or my family about Sergei's warning that someone may try to kidnap me as leverage. I figured if I kept to safe places, then I wouldn't need to. Telling Rafe or my father and brothers would only result in my not being able to leave the house at *all*, and I knew I couldn't cope with that.

Not for the first time, I was incredibly thankful Katya had stumbled her way into my life. Though she hadn't been too keen on keeping the potential kidnapping part of Sergei's theory secret, she understood why I wanted things to be that way and had respected my decision. It was one of the few decisions left for me to make.

And so it was I took a walk to the local grocery store for some ice cream. It was a hot, suffocating afternoon, and it was Clara's day off. With the feeling that I was being followed still clinging to my skin, I didn't like it at all, but I couldn't see where on Earth such a stalker could be.

There were no cars on the road. The cars parked along the edge of the sidewalk were empty, and the people I walked past on the street were busy going about their lives. Nobody was hanging outside the shops. Nobody had furtive eyes obsessively watching the area.

For all intents and purposes, I was not being followed.

God, I needed to sleep. Or maybe get drunk. I just needed to get out of my head, even if only for a few hours. I guess I'd have to settle for a triple chocolate ice cream instead.

Ice cream in hand, I tried my best to clear my mind as I walked back to my father's house. It was only a ten-minute walk in a neighborhood I knew like the back of my hand. Nobody would be crazy enough to stalk me here.

And yet...

I turned around sharply. Something didn't feel right. But there was nobody around, which may have just been exacerbating my fears. It was all I could do to stop myself from running full on all the way home.

When finally I did make it to my front door, I almost walked straight into Rafe.

"Rafe! I wasn't expecting to see you today," I exclaimed, aware of my heart hammering away in my chest.

He raised an eyebrow at me. "I was surprised you weren't in. I actually stopped by to discuss something with your dad, but obviously, I wanted to see you, too."

"Good to know I'm playing second fiddle to my old man."

Rafe let out a laugh. "What were you up to?"

"Buying ice cream. Care to join me for some in the garden?"

He glanced at his watch, then smiled. "I have a half-hour to spare. Why not?"

I breathed a sigh of relief at his answer. Sitting in the garden with Rafe and a pint of frozen dairy goodness was the most normal thing I'd been able to do in weeks. We reclined in lounge chairs, sharing a spoon between us as we ate straight from the carton. Rafe took his suit jacket off and loosened his tie to better take in the sunshine.

In the deep, rich late-afternoon sunshine, I saw how tired he was. His face was haggard and ashen.

"You haven't been sleeping much either, huh?"

He looked at me with worry. "No, but this will hopefully be over sooner rather than later, and then the two of us will be able to sleep like the dead until we feel normal again."

There was silence for a few moments as we continued to eat ice cream and look around the garden, watching birds flit to the feeders and a stray cat crawl through the underbrush to try to catch one of them.

"I think I'm being followed, Rafe."

I didn't look at him when I said it. I kept my eyes straight ahead. In my peripheral, I noticed him freeze up for a second, but then he relaxed.

"It's normal to feel like that, given everything that's going on."

"So you think I'm being crazy?"

"No, I think you're exhausted and stressed and well within your rights to believe someone is following you."

"But you don't personally think anyone is, do you?"

"No. They'd be insane to try to stalk you around these parts. It's not logical."

I knew everything Rafe was saying was exactly what I'd been thinking, but not having him even entertain the idea that someone was stalking me kind of stung. Why would he not believe me? Did he honestly think I was being paranoid?

I stood up abruptly.

"You're right. I'm tired. I'm going to head upstairs to try to sleep. Bye, Rafe."

"Kirsten."

I held out a hand as he made to stand up. "Don't 'Kirsten' me. It's fine. You should probably get some sleep yourself. You look awful."

I ran back into the house before Rafe could say anything else, leaving my half-eaten tub of ice cream to melt underneath the blazing sun. When I collapsed onto my bed, I was ashamed to feel tears pooling in my eyes.

Rafe was supposed to believe me. After everything we'd been through—after growing up together and falling in love with each other and planning to run away together—he should have believed me.

The man who had been speaking to me downstairs hadn't been my Rafe. It was lawyer Rafe. Lately, that was the only version of him I saw. It upset me to no end. I didn't know how to handle lawyer Rafe.

I kept waiting for a knock on my door, accompanied by Rafe's voice gently asking me to let him in, but it never came. What the hell was going on? Why was he freezing me out? Was he really just being professional until the case was over? It certainly didn't feel that way.

Maybe I was being neurotic and tired. Ugh, I hated him. And I hated myself. This wasn't how things were supposed to be.

A call on my phone shocked me out of my hate spiral.

"Have you made it your life's purpose to scare the living daylights out of me with phone calls, Dean Collins?" I asked when I answered the phone.

"Not intentionally, but that sounds pretty appealing," he replied, though he sounded uncharacteristically serious.

I frowned. "What's up?"

"We've had a suspicious customer in the last few days. Actually, he came in once or twice asking for you personally a few weeks ago, but you hadn't been in the clinic, so I didn't even think to mention it to you. When he came in this time, he wasn't asking for you, which was odd. He brought in a cat he said was having some stomach problems. Thing is, I distinctly remember a woman coming in telling me her cat had been stolen and to look out for it if I could."

"Definitely the same cat?"

"Definitely. She gave me some photos—the cat's markings match exactly."

"If he wasn't asking for me this time, what was he doing?"

"That's the thing, I'm not sure. I think he might have been looking for something. I'm wondering if he has something to do with the drug charges against you. He may have been trying to get his hands on some of our supply."

"Did you say anything to him about the cat?"

"I told him yesterday I'd need to keep it in overnight to run some tests but he could pick up the cat this afternoon. He never showed. I think he's on to me."

"Do you have any evidence he was snooping about?"

"I'm just looking through the CCTV footage now. Should I send it over to Rafe or the detective working your case?"

"No," I replied, a little too quickly and forcefully. "No. Send it to me. It might be nothing. I should at least see if I recognize him first."

Dean didn't sound altogether convinced. "If you're sure."

"Definitely. Did he give a name?"

"John Rogers, but I'm pretty sure it's fake. I didn't think to press him about it at the time."

"That's no problem, Dean. Thanks for letting me know."

"O'Leary…be careful."

"What do you mean?"

"It's just," he let out a weary sigh, "I'm worried this guy

might be following you or is looking for you. Have you seen anyone suspicious around your neighborhood lately?"

"I—I haven't seen anyone, but I honestly feel like someone is following me. I thought I was going crazy."

"Don't say that. There's every reason to believe that's exactly what's happening right now. You've got to be extra vigilant, okay?"

And just like that, Dean believed me. He didn't throw my worries away or pin them on neurotic delusions.

Why couldn't Rafe do that?

I smiled slightly. "I will. Don't worry—I was double checking every street corner before I went round it already."

"That's going a little far," he laughed, "though I wouldn't be against you locking yourself up in your father's house until this all blows over."

"As if."

"Well, if you're not going to be contained, are we still on for dinner tomorrow? Rose can make it, too, and I'm sure between the three of us in a public space, we could ward off any wannabe stalkers."

"Hilarious. Yes, I'm in; God knows I need a break."

"Good to hear. Right, I best get back to work. Another double shift courtesy of a certain someone being unable to work right now."

"Way to drive a spear through my heart."

"Anytime, O'Leary."

"I hope you get a horrible patient in this evening," I teased, then hung up the phone to the sound of him laughing.

I rolled over onto my back on my bed, staring at my blank cell phone screen for way too long. Dean had known me less than two years, and he had no trouble believing me. Rafe had known me all my life, and he doubted me.

Where had I gone wrong? What did I need to do or say to make him believe me? Should I have told him about what Sergei had said?

It wasn't as if I wanted to be locked up in the house, which was what would happen if I told Rafe about what Sergei thought might happen. All I wanted was for him to believe me, and to—I didn't know. Just be by my side, making sure I was safe, I guess. Was that too much to ask?

Apparently so.

With regret, I realized I'd left my ice cream outside. Groaning, I hauled myself away from my bed and lumbered down the stairs and outside to retrieve the melted, sticky mess before a fox or the birds could get to it. I noticed Rafe had left his suit jacket folded on the back of the chair.

"How thoughtless of him…" I murmured as I picked it up and took it back inside with me up to my room. It smelled of him, which meant it smelled amazing.

If he wanted it back, he could come and get it back from me armed with an apology—and more ice cream.

But until then, it was mine. It was a subpar replacement for the man himself, but given the situation I was in, I wasn't in a position to complain. Not caring if I rumpled up the material, I curled into a ball on my bed with the jacket in hand, breathing in Rafe's smell as I finally felt myself falling asleep.

CHAPTER TWENTY

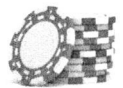

Lying was taking more than just a physical toll on me. It was wearing me down mentally, and hard. Having to tell Kirsten she wasn't being followed when she clearly was had been the most difficult lie I'd uttered so far.

But I knew Kirsten O'Leary. If she knew someone was stalking her, she'd actively try to find them. She'd look around every street corner, inside every car, into every shop, trying to work out who was watching her. I couldn't blame her for it. It was in her nature. Her father wanted eyes on her, but Kirsten said the only concession she'd make was to stay at the family home. Lord knows if they didn't agree, she'd find herself in more trouble. Kirsten and trouble went together like peanut butter and jelly. You couldn't have one without the other.

Given what I knew about Brian Feldman, I wasn't in a position to risk Kirsten's safety by allowing her to follow her nature. If I could get away with locking her inside the O'Leary household, you could be damn sure I would, but Kirsten would undoubtedly find a way to sneak out. After all—she'd done it many times before.

None of that made me feel any better. Watching her face crumple with disappointment right in front of me when she realized I didn't believe her had been heartbreaking. The way she ran away from me to hide inside her room. I'd wanted nothing more than to follow her and explain everything.

Then I saw Ian speaking with his father and thought better of it. The look the two men had given me was reason enough to stay quiet.

That led to me trying to drown my sorrows in a glass of whiskey. It was the good stuff Kirsten had left at my house, which of course made me feel worse. When I heard the front door open and close and the sound of Matt's voice saying goodbye on the phone, I almost got up to mull over things in my room, just to be alone. But I didn't. I didn't have the energy to move.

"Jesus, Rafe, you look awful," Matt said in lieu of a greeting when he entered the kitchen.

"You're not the first person to say that to me today."

Matt sat down beside me and joined me in pouring a glass of whiskey, uncharacteristically silent for once. He kept glancing at me out of the corner of his eye until eventually, my patience cracked.

"What the hell is it, Matt?"

He looked away uncomfortably. "Katya told me something

about the meeting with Sergei—I mean, we tell each other everything, but she didn't want you to know because Kirsten had made her promise not to say—"

"Just tell me," I interrupted, rubbing my temple. Kirsten had kept something from me about her meeting with Sergei, despite me expressly saying in no uncertain terms was she to keep anything from me.

"Sergei told her it was likely the members of the Russian mob he imagined being responsible for the drug charges against Kirsten would try to kidnap her so they could blame it on Sergei."

I stared at my brother, bug-eyed. "And you're only telling me this now?" Kirsten had been worried she was being followed if she'd heard that. If she was being stalked by both the Russian mob and Brian Feldman…oh holy hell.

She wasn't as safe in this neighborhood as I'd thought. If the two groups were working together, as Liam O'Leary had hypothesized, we were screwed.

I needed to tell Detective Peters. I needed to talk to Sergei. I needed to—

I needed to see Kirsten. I'd been an asshole to her in my desperation to act purely as her lawyer. I needed to comfort her and tell her I believed her. With the Russian mob possibly out to kidnap her, I needn't even mention Feldman to her. I could support her without raising suspicion or the wrath of her family.

Matt gave me a knowing look. "Don't drive if you've been drinking."

"I only had the one," I replied as I threw my shoes back on, grabbed my keys and left.

I was parked on the street outside of the O'Leary house before I knew it. I didn't want anyone else in her family to know I was there. All I wanted to do was see Kirsten. Luckily, I'd spent long enough with her to know a thing or two about sneaking in and out of her house.

Grinning at the memory of doing this exact same thing in our teen years, I hoisted myself up and over the garden wall closest to Kirsten's window using a trellis to climb up the side of the house. Jesus, this was so much harder now that I was a grown man. I struggled my way up to her windowsill. Luckily, the window was open.

Thanking the late-summer heaviness for the open window, I slid through the gap as silently as possible and into Kirsten's room.

She was sound asleep on top of her bed, curled around my suit jacket. It was only in looking at the heartwarming scene in front of me that I realized I'd forgotten it earlier in the garden. Quietly, I took off my shoes and padded over to sit by Kirsten's head. I ran a gentle hand through her hair, rubbing my fingertips against her scalp until she began to stir.

"Kirsten, it's me," I murmured.

Her eyelashes fluttered sleepily as she replied, "Rafe? Is that you?"

She tried to sit up, still barely conscious, as she blinked her eyes. I nudged her back down as I climbed on top of the bed to curl up beside her.

"What are you doing here?" she asked, more awake now. There was a tiny frown creasing her brow. I leaned in and kissed it away, but the frown only turned more pronounced. "That wasn't very professional."

"I'm not here as your lawyer. I'm here as Rafe. Your Rafe."

"Why can't they be the same person?"

"They just—can't, Kirsten. My interest in you as a man and as your lawyer are different."

She looked downcast. "I know that, but it doesn't stop it from stinging."

"You should have told me everything Sergei said, you idiot."

Now, that caught Kirsten's attention.

"Katya told you?"

"Matt did. Apparently, they tell each other everything, and Matt couldn't keep it from me. You should have told me, especially if you were convinced you were being followed."

She shoved a hand against my chest. "You should have believed me, regardless. And I didn't want you to lock me up for fear of me looking for the stalker."

"At least you're aware of your own stupidity." I laughed softly, grasping hold of her hand before she could pull it back. I kissed each of her fingertips one by one by one. I was happy to see her blush.

"You're hiding something from me, aren't you?" she asked suddenly, studying my face carefully in case I was about to lie.

"Yes. I have to."

"Then it's hypocritical of you to suggest I shouldn't hide things from you."

"I know. I need to keep some things from you, nonetheless. Just for now. When this is over—"

"Everyone keeps saying that. 'When this is over'. Well, guess what? I have to live this whole thing right now. Who knows how long this damn case will take? What if my name gets cleared but the actual culprits are never caught? Who's to say—"

I kissed her. I reached in and swallowed the rest of her fears with my lips, not knowing what else to do or say. There was nothing left to say.

"Rafe, what are you doing?" she asked breathlessly. "I thought you said we had to wait?"

I didn't break away from her gaze as I replied, "That was before. But you're right, we're living in the present, so what the hell am I doing not actually living it? Kirsten, I love you. And you know that. I'm tired of hiding it."

I was aware it was the first time I'd told her I loved her out loud. There was a certain relief and euphoria to it. Especially when she smiled in delight.

"I love you, too."

And then there really was nothing left to say. There were only actions.

My lips found hers again as her hands made quick work of my tie, then the buttons of my shirt, and then my belt. My hands slid around her back and undid her bra, and in one swift motion, I pulled her dress up and over her head, taking the undergarment with it.

"I haven't seen you this naked since we were little kids playing in a paddling pool," I joked as I took in the sight of her bare, beautiful breasts in the moonlight. They were beautiful—*she* was beautiful—and a rapidly hardening sensation in my pants seemed to agree with me.

"Such a dick," she muttered as she ran her hands over my arms, removing my shirt as she pulled me on top of her, kissing me passionately. She hooked her legs around my waist, grinding against me until it was almost painful to keep my pants on.

I broke away from her just long enough to remove the rest of my clothes, then slid her panties off with one hand, keeping my eyes on her the whole time.

"I take back what I said earlier," she said as I straddled her, taking in the entirely perfect sight of Kirsten naked beneath me.

"What do you mean?"

She laughed a little. "I said you looked awful. You absolutely don't. You're sexy as hell, Rafe. Tell me why we didn't do this sooner."

"Because…I'm an idiot."

"That you are," she agreed as she pulled me back down and crushed her lips against mine.

And then we were hands through hair, lips on skin, tangled limbs and flashes of pleasure as we explored each other's bodies, desperate and hungry and mad for each other. We didn't stop. We couldn't. It was only as the sky began to lighten across the horizon that, finally, the two of us collapsed onto the bed, spent and exhausted.

We didn't sleep for long. In fact, it felt as if we'd barely slept at all when my cell phone buzzed, informing me I needed to get up for work. It took me a moment to remember it was Saturday and I had no work to go to. Happily, I turned off the alarm and rolled over to nestle back against her.

Her sleeping face was blissful in the morning light. Without thinking, I reached in and kissed her lips. Kirsten moaned slightly and reciprocated before pulling away.

"What time is it?" she mumbled, eyes still closed as she stretched.

"Just after seven. Go back to sleep."

"I will if you will," she replied, a happy smile on her face. God, I could get used to this. Waking up next to Kirsten was unbearably addictive—and this was the first time it had happened.

"I love you."

She opened her eyes, the sun glinting off her green irises as if she belonged to a clan of woodland elves. She kissed the end of my nose.

"I love you, too."

We were startled out of the moment by a noise in the hallway. Kirsten was immediately wide awake.

"Shit, my brothers stayed last night. That'll be Ian getting up."

"It's not as if he'll come in here at seven in the morning, will he?"

"No, but Clara might, and I don't want you to be around when that happens. She'll make some comment that Ian will latch on to and take way too far."

I chuckled under my breath. "Yeah, I guess you're right. Okay, I'll head out the way I came in. Can I see you tonight?" I asked as I retrieved my clothes from the floor.

"Ah, I'm meeting Dean and Rose tonight for dinner, but maybe after that?"

"You still have that curfew, so just let me know when you get home, and if I feel like entertaining you, I'll swing by."

She pouted. "That's cruel."

"So is you meeting Dean for dinner."

"And Rose. Besides, I'm going to tell him no. He'd wanted me to wait until everything had blown over, but that's not fair to him. My feelings won't change. He's just a friend."

I raised an eyebrow.

"A good friend, yes, but a friend nonetheless. He's been so supportive with absolutely zero ulterior motives this whole time. So get over the jealousy."

I laughed as I put my tie back on. "I'll consider it."

She walked over and kissed me. "I'll see you later, then."

I'd never felt as much regret as I did in that moment, watching a naked Kirsten in the morning sunlight get further and further away as I descended from her window. I gave her a wave once I hit the garden, turned around and took a solid three steps before I walked straight into Ian.

"Shit," I let out inadvertently.

Ian took one look at me, then Kirsten's window, where she'd hidden behind a curtain and punched me in the face.

"You son of a bitch!" he roared as I recoiled from the punch. "You son of a bitch," he repeated. "Where do you get off sneaking into my sister's bedroom like some damn pervert, then running off in the morning? Who the hell do you think you are?"

"Ian, stop for a second—"

"Don't you dare tell me to stop. Here I was thinking maybe, just maybe you were serious and respectful enough this time around that it might be okay. You were keeping professional while being her lawyer; you were doing everything right; you were putting in the effort with my dad—but no. You just had to go and sleep with my sister behind my back."

"Ian—"

"Get the hell out of here!" he screamed, swinging to hit me again. "Just get the hell away."

I didn't stick around long enough for him to connect a second punch with the side of my face. I vaulted over the garden wall and ran straight for my car, driving home as fast as I could without breaking the speed limit.

I shouldn't have done that. I shouldn't have gone behind my best friend's back in the worst way possible.

And yet.

And yet.

I didn't regret what had happened between Kirsten and me.

The *way* it had happened, yes, but not the fact it had happened. The minute I sank into her body, it was perfect. The way she clung to me as if I was the only person left on Earth. That was heavenly. I didn't regret the act; just the exit.

"Guess I'll add making amends with Ian onto the list of things I need to fix," I muttered aloud. The high from sleeping with Kirsten rapidly disintegrated as the reality of our lives came crashing back around me.

But now I knew. I knew exactly what I could have with Kirsten when everything was over, and it was intoxicating. Especially when I received a text message from her.

Sorry about Ian. I'll deal with it. Love you.

If ever I was going to catch the assholes who were after Kirsten, it was now.

I had run out of patience. They were going down.

CHAPTER TWENTY-ONE

There was nothing like finally sleeping with the man you loved then watching your brother try to beat him up to make you crave alcohol. Thank God for Rose and Dean. It had been a long, painful day to get through from the moment I witnessed my brother punching Rafe in the face to the moment I finally got to leave for dinner.

Luckily for me, my father hadn't wanted to hear anything Ian had to say on the matter.

"What's between Rafe and Kirsten is between Rafe and Kirsten, Ian," he'd said, "even if the way he entered and exited the house leaves something to be desired. Regardless of how unprofessional it was, that was no excuse for punching him in the face."

My father had looked at me as if he'd expected better of me but otherwise said nothing. Given my situation, what would he suggest Rafe and I do instead? The fact that he didn't say anything to me spoke volumes. I could make my own decisions, and it wasn't his place to weigh in on the matter.

The fact that he was treating me as an adult when Rafe and I had basically acted like kids made me feel pretty awful. And yet still…

How could I regret what had happened? I'd loved every moment of it. I could deal with Rafe keeping secrets for the time being, just so long as we could be as close as we'd been last night. It had been—I didn't know how to describe it. Electric, maybe. Frenetic, even.

Perfect, definitely.

I glanced at Dean, who was carelessly laughing away at a comment Rose had made. I didn't want to have to hurt his feelings, but ultimately I had to do the right thing. I had to do *the adult thing*. I had to turn him down.

Just not while Rose was around to bear witness to the whole thing.

"Three more screwdrivers, please," I asked the bartender of the bar we'd found ourselves in after dinner. It was called Ringo's, a bar that played classic 60s rock, situated about five minutes from Capone's. It had been Dean's eclectic choice. He'd been unapologetic about it.

"What, so I like the Beach Boys, Beatles and Bob Dylan—get over it," he'd said when we arrived.

I didn't mind in the slightest. It was good to try new places, and once I got over the initial strangeness of it, I found myself thoroughly enjoying the music, especially when I began recognizing some songs as favorites from my father's childhood. Rose had protested, of course—60s rock was definitely not her style, but she'd drunk enough alcohol to be swayed otherwise.

I hadn't realized how much I needed a night out until I was in it. I still had my curfew, so in reality, it was only just past nine. It frustrated me that I would have to leave in under an hour, but I decided not to dwell on that.

Besides, I could call Rafe over when I got back home, Ian be damned. Rafe could apologize to my father for having snuck in through my window, and everything would be fine.

But first I had to turn Dean down. I waited for Rose to need the restroom, but by God, the girl had the bladder of a camel. She hadn't gone once, not even at dinner.

Rose smiled bashfully when I handed over her drink from the bartender. "Thanks, Kirst—but this *definitely* has to be my last one. I'm on call tomorrow."

"Sucks to be you," I threw at her as I similarly threw vodka and orange juice down my throat.

Dean laughed. "Somebody's in a very good mood, O'Leary. Something nice happen?"

"You could—you could say that," I stammered. The expression on Dean's face froze—for just a second. But it was enough. I could tell.

He knew.

And then he smiled his easy smile. "God knows you

deserve something good to happen to you, given how hellish your life has been the past few weeks."

"You're telling me."

Just like that, the conversation returned to normal. I knew I had to say something a little more official to Dean, but it could wait until we were alone. For now, I was content with letting us have a good time.

We were all shocked when a man snaked his arms around Rose's waist. "Guess who?" he announced.

"What the hell—" she began, then squealed in delight when she turned around. "Josh. Oh my God. What are you doing here?"

Josh grinned from ear to ear. "You'll never guess what, babe, but my transfer went through."

"When?"

"Three days ago, but I wanted to surprise you."

Rose let out another noise of glee as she threw her arms around him, then turned back to us. "Dean, Kirsten, this is my boyfriend, Joshua. I'm sorry to do this, but I'm definitely getting the hell out of this place with him this very second."

It was only then Rose finally took a trip to the restroom, then left with her boyfriend back to her apartment, leaving me and Dean alone. While I'd wanted an opportunity to speak to him by himself all evening, now that the opportunity had been thrust upon me, I didn't know what to say.

"That's really—that's so good that Josh got a job in Vegas," I said, desperate for something to talk about. "I was worried Rose would have to move back over, but this is great."

"Just don't leave, Kirsten."

"Huh?" I stared at Dean, who regarded me seriously.

"I can tell I've lost to Rafe. That's okay. I'm glad I don't have to regret never telling you how I felt. But don't leave."

"Don't leave?"

"Vegas. The clinic. Me." He smiled wistfully. "Not in an awkward way or anything. I'll get over my feelings for you. But—" Dean paused for a moment, downing his drink before continuing. "You must know I equally regard you as a good friend and a particularly great colleague. I couldn't bear losing you to another clinic."

I didn't know what to say. It reminded me that I'd been thinking just the same thing a week ago—that I didn't want to leave Vegas.

My answer was so easy.

"You're not getting rid of me so easily, Dr. Collins," I replied, a stupid grin on my face that contradicted the fact that I felt close to tears. "I'm here to stay, like it or not."

I was suddenly caught in a crushing embrace. Dean leaned his head on my shoulder as I gasped in surprise.

"Just for a moment. I swear, just for a moment, and then you never need to deal with a pining forty-year-old man again."

"You're thirty-eight. There's life in you yet."

He laughed raucously as he pulled away from me. "Okay, I'm heading to the restroom for a moment. Not to cry, so don't even suggest I am. Then one more drink, and that'll be you hitting curfew, so I'll make sure you get home okay."

"Thanks, Dean."

That left me nursing the dregs of my drink at the bar, alone. The bar wasn't exactly quiet, so I was content to bask in the sounds of other people enjoying their Saturday night and the final minute of "Hey Jude".

"So I'm a little older than forty, but care to entertain another pining middle-aged man?" came a voice from my left. I turned to regard the speaker—a man who looked similar in age to my father. He was unassuming in appearance, with graying brown hair and muddy brown eyes to match, though he was clearly tall despite the way he stooped his shoulders.

"Can I help you?" I asked politely though I was immediately on edge. I felt like I recognized the man from somewhere. Not that I'd met him before, rather I'd seen him in passing in a photograph or video or something, but I couldn't place him.

It made me feel uncomfortable.

The man smiled, but it didn't really reach his eyes. "I don't think so. All I wanted to do was buy you a drink. I've been watching you for a while."

What a creep, I thought as I looked the other way.

"Um, no, thank you. I'm actually just waiting for my friend to return from the restroom, and then we're leaving."

"That's such a shame. I really wanted to get to know you better. My name's Brian Feldman," he said, holding out his hand to me.

Reluctantly, I shook his hand, willing Dean to hurry the hell up. I wanted to leave.

"Nice to—nice to meet you, Brian," I stammered, trying to release my hand from his, but his grip only tightened. His smile turned into a distorted, grotesque grin.

"You're not going anywhere, Kirsten O'Leary."

And then I recognized him. He was the man from Dean's CCTV footage.

I tried harder to break free and managed to move about a foot or two toward the door, but he grabbed me around the waist and held me against him.

"Let me go!" I screamed, alerting the rest of the bar to my predicament. A few people got up to come to my aid, but then several men stood up with guns, eliciting screams and cries from the bar-goers.

I recognized one or two of them from my role as the mob doctor—members of the Russian mob.

Ah, shit.

Sergei's suspicions had turned out to be right on the money, but who the hell was this late middle-aged man who was working with them, currently holding me tightly and preventing me from leaving?

When Dean returned from the restroom, it was with horror I realized what was going to happen. He recognized the danger and charged over to my rescue without thinking, then Brian shot him. The man shot Dean, who fell to the floor in a crumpled heap.

"No!" I kept screaming as Brian dragged me out of the bar,

the members of the Russian mob following closely behind. I kept thinking of things I should have done.

I should have stayed at my father's house.

I should have told Rafe about Sergei's suspicions earlier.

I should have called Rafe and met him earlier.

Rafe.

I needed Rafe.

As they dragged me into a car, I saw Dean, bleeding from a wound in his stomach, dragging himself out of the bar after me.

Brian shot him again.

"Son of a bitch should have stayed down," he muttered as he slammed me into the back of a car, slid in beside me, and closed the door.

He turned to face me, looking me up and down with a critical expression on his face.

Then he made a noise of disgust. "I can't believe you have his damn eyes."

CHAPTER TWENTY-TWO

There were several people you could expect to call you at ten in the evening on a Saturday. Your spouse, for example. Or a hook-up. Maybe your boss if there was an emergency at the office.

One of the last people I expected to get a call from at ten in the evening on a Saturday was my rival for Kirsten O'Leary's affections—Dean. Curious about what he could possibly need to tell me so late, I picked up.

"Dean? I take it there's a good reason for this."

"Kirsten—gone," Dean interrupted, his voice and breath ragged and labored. I bolted upright from my slumped position in my late father's study. Something was seriously wrong.

"Dean, what happened? Where are you? Are you hurt?"

"Shot. Ambulance on its way. Call that…that detective on Kirsten's case. Kidnapped. She's been kidnapped."

My blood ran cold. "Where are you right now? I'm on my way."

"Outside…outside Ringo's—five minutes from Capone's."

"Got it. Dean, stay conscious. Don't you dare close your eyes. I'll be there as soon as I can."

"Get her—get her back."

The line went dead as Dean hung up.

For one horrible, drawn-out moment, I stood motionless and numb. My stomach heaved and roiled, and I thought I might be sick. Someone had taken Kirsten. Someone had taken her, and I hadn't been there to stop it.

Self-pity could wait. I hurriedly threw on my jacket and screamed for my brother, who'd been hanging out at the house more than usual. No doubt concerned for me.

"Matt. I need you. Have Katya call the O'Learys and meet me at Capone's."

Matt was by my side and ready to leave in under thirty seconds, Katya not far behind.

"What happened?" she asked nervously after seeing the look on my face.

I couldn't say it, but I had to.

"Kirsten's been kidnapped."

Matt's face went from shock, to sympathy, to outright snarling rage. "Then we'll get her back. Katya—"

"Call Sergei," she interrupted immediately. "Got it. I'll get the rest of the O'Learys, too, Rafe, just…go."

Matt drove. I couldn't trust my shaking hands behind the

wheel. Thank God we were just a couple minutes drive from Ringo's.

I pulled out my cell phone and called Detective Peters.

"Charles, you need to get to Ringo's now," I shouted into the phone as soon as the man picked up.

"We just sent a full police unit over there. Someone called in an armed kidnapping."

"It was Kirsten," I interrupted. "They took Kirsten. They shot her friend."

There was a pause. "I'll be there in five."

"I'll see you in three," I said, trying to get him to hurry.

I hung up, drumming my fingers against my leg in a frantic, impatient manner as we got stuck behind a line of traffic. I couldn't begin to process what Dean had said. Everything so far was somehow still just words.

Kirsten had been taken even after trying to keep her in a safe neighborhood, having her stay at home, and rarely letting her be alone. She'd been taken when she was out with her friends, in public, in a bustling bar on a Saturday night.

The futility of the situation struck me. Was there nothing any of us could have done to prevent this? Had I been there with Kirsten would I have been able to save her? Or would I have ended up with a bullet inside me, like Dean?

My stomach twisted. Dean hadn't sounded good. I prayed, for his sake and for Kirsten's, he wouldn't die.

Come on, Dean, you can't vie for Kirsten's affections from the grave, I thought, knowing it didn't matter what I thought. Either he would live or he wouldn't.

It should have been me. Regardless of whether I could have prevented Kirsten's kidnapping or not, I should have been there with her this evening. I should have been more insistent about meeting up with her. I merely asked her where she would be going for drinks after dinner. I could have been there.

It was too late. She was gone.

I threw myself out of Matt's car before he'd finished pulling up. There was a small crowd outside of Ringo's. In the distance, I could hear the sound of the ambulance sirens. I pushed through the crowd and collapsed beside Dean. He was ashen and bloody. Someone was keeping pressure on two separate bullet wounds. One on his shoulder and one right through his stomach.

But no heart or lung punctures, I thought as I scanned the man's body. That had to be a good thing.

"Dean, it's Rafe," I called out to him, grabbing on to the man's hand to make him aware of my presence. He barely opened his eyes.

"My phone," he muttered, glancing down at his pocket. "Password's 1763."

I didn't waste time. I located the phone and unlocked it, staring back at him for further instructions.

"File—video file—first one."

With shaking hands, I searched Dean's phone until I brought up his video gallery, stabbing the first file open with a finger. It was CCTV footage of the vet clinic—of Brian Feldman.

Dean's eyes roved underneath his eyelids. "He took her. That man...took her."

Liam O'Leary's worst fears had come to light. Feldman had kidnapped his daughter.

"Dean, why did you never tell me about this footage?" I asked the man frantically. "I've been looking for him."

How could Dean have known that? I had told no one but Detective Peters.

"Kirsten didn't want you to—to worry. Thought it was nothing. Ha...last time I listen to that idiot."

The ambulance reached us then, the paramedics taking over as they put Dean on oxygen and hauled him into the back of the ambulance.

"I'll get her back," I shouted over to him just as the doors began to close behind him. "Don't you dare die."

If he died, I would never be able to forgive myself. I'd never be able to look Kirsten in the eye again.

A hand on my shoulder startled me, but it was only Matt.

"Rafe, Detective Peters is here."

Charles rushed over. "I got the lowdown from some witnesses. A late middle-aged man apprehended Kirsten O'Leary with the help of several members of the Russian mob."

"It was Feldman."

Charles frowned. "You're certain?"

I showed him the CCTV footage from Dean's phone. "Dean Collins—the man who was shot—confirmed it was the man in this video. Come with me to Capone's, Charles."

"Who are we meeting?"

"Sergei Volkov and Liam O'Leary."

"Rafe, we need to be careful to stay on the right side of the law here," he said.

I stared at the man, bug-eyed.

"You think I don't know that? We can worry about that after we find Kirsten. In order to find her, Sergei and Liam are our best shots."

Charles' lips thinned. "Lead the way, then."

When Matt, Charles and I reached Capone's, Katya flung herself into Matt's arms as Ian looked at me, his face devoid of any emotion. He looked hollow.

"Where is my baby sister?" he asked nobody in particular. I'd never seen Ian like this. It was terrible. I wished he were seething and foaming from the mouth, ready to punch me in the face for allowing this to happen. Anything but seeing him broken.

Patrick moved forwards to shake hands with Charles. "Patrick O'Leary," he said. "You must be Detective Peters. What can you tell us about what happened at Ringo's?"

I let Charles take the lead, explaining to Ian, Patrick, and their silent father about what had happened.

Sergei showed up just as Charles completed his explanation.

"I know where those traitorous assholes will be," he announced in lieu of an introduction. I was sincerely grateful the man was straight to the point. "There's a warehouse just off the road on the way to the Calico Basin that seems likely.

My bodyguard is working on getting the exact location out of one of the co-conspirators we caught earlier, but I'm fairly sure it's this warehouse."

Liam shook his head. "I think I have a better idea of where Feldman is. His family were always long-time members of Canyon Gate and had some private rooms there."

I swung my head between the two of them. "Do you think the Russian mob may have broken away from Feldman once the kidnapping was completed?"

Sergei looked thoughtful for a moment. "No. I think they'll still be together. I found a connection to one of Yuri's minions. He did time with Feldman. Heard Feldman stopped an attack, so they owed him."

Now it all made sense. I couldn't put together how a guy like Feldman could influence Russian mobsters, but debts were always paid.

I glanced at Charles. "Do we have grounds to check Canyon Gate without a warrant?"

He shook his head. "Not exactly, but I'm friends with the manager. He'll let us in."

"Then we go to this warehouse via Canyon Gate and check them both out."

"I have men on their way over to the warehouse already as backup," Sergei added.

"I have men over checking out Canyon Gate already, too," Liam said.

Charles groaned. "If I catch any of them doing anything illegal, you know I'll have to arrest them."

"If you catch them," just about everybody else said at the same time.

"This is why I need to retire," Charles said. "Far too much organized crime in Vegas for my liking."

We split into two cars. I made sure I was sitting with Ian, who remained quiet.

"Ian, I—"

"I don't care," he interrupted. "Who gives a shit about you climbing through the damn window if Kirsten's been taken? If we get her back, then I don't give a damn what the two of you do together."

It was the worst situation in which to get Ian's approval, yet I appreciated it nonetheless.

When we finally reached Canyon Gate, it was to our complete surprise that Kirsten, Feldman, and the Russian mob members were nowhere to be seen.

That meant all our hopes were now pinned on how well Sergei knew his men, traitorous or otherwise.

I couldn't believe I had to rely on the Russian mob to save my woman. So much for us getting out of this life for good. If we could save her, then I didn't care how we did it, who we used, or what I'd owe.

CHAPTER TWENTY-THREE

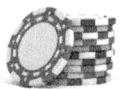

I didn't know where I was being taken. The windows of the car I was in were opaque. I couldn't see a thing. Not that it would have helped me all that much to know where I was going. The man named Brian Feldman had taken my phone and thrown it out of the window only a minute or two after we left the bar.

I wasn't sure what to do. Brian hadn't said a word since we drove off, not even to explain the comment he'd made about my eyes. Who on Earth was he? What did he have to do with the Russian mob? I didn't understand. Nothing added up.

After a while, the car came to a stop and I was pulled out of the back seat and roughly dragged by the arm into a warehouse. I had no clue where we were. I didn't recognize a thing.

The space was dark and empty. Large, overhead lights flickered on as I was made to follow one of the members of the Russian mob over to a group of pallets stacked high with televisions. Two men rolled one of them to the side, revealing a concealed door recessed into the floor. When they opened it, it became clear they intended to force me through it, I started to scream until a hand slid around my mouth to silence me.

"I don't think so," Brian whispered into my ear before flinging me unceremoniously through the trapdoor.

I tumbled down some stairs, hitting the floor with a dull thud and sharp twinge of pain. I'd landed badly on my right leg. My hope rapidly drained away as I realized I wouldn't be able to run off now even if I miraculously had the opportunity to do so.

"What am I gonna do?" I breathed aloud, the words barely audible as the door above me slammed shut.

I was left in pitch darkness for an immeasurable about of time. It could have been five minutes. It could just as easily have been five hours.

I kept my eyes closed as I tried to calm myself. If this really was the end, if this was where I would die, at least I had told Rafe I loved him. At least we were together. At least I had my family's blessing to go ahead with the relationship even if Ian was still being as overbearing as an older brother could be. At least I'd gotten to know my long-lost sister. At least I'd sorted things out with Dean.

Dean. My heart hurt as much as my leg when I thought about Dean lying in a bloody, crumpled mess on the sidewalk outside Ringo's. I prayed to God he was still alive.

I reassured myself someone would have called an ambulance. If Dean could be saved, he would be.

Did Rafe know what was going on? Surely, by this point, Detective Peters would have found out the woman who was kidnapped was me and subsequently alerted Rafe and my family. I could only hope, but what could they do ultimately? None of them had any clue where I was.

And still, I had to cling to the idea that they were desperately looking for me, even as I sat here wondering whether my damaged leg could bear any weight.

I stood up to test it. My leg immediately buckled beneath me.

Okay, not broken, but horribly sprained, I concluded as I massaged my ankle, cringing at the pain. If push came to shove, then maybe with enough adrenaline in my system I could sprint out of here.

But again—to where? Even with my eyes slowly adjusting to the darkness, there was no obvious way out. I was in a basement. Other than the set of stairs leading up to the trapdoor and two metal-framed chairs by the back wall, the room was empty.

I hauled one of the chairs over and sat on it. The bare, concrete floor had been cold and uncomfortable. The metal chair wasn't much better, but at least I could smash it into someone's face if I needed to.

When the trapdoor finally opened, the light spilling down from above obscured the figure descending the stairs until they located a light switch I couldn't possibly have found in the dark. They closed the door behind them, leaving me trapped once more.

It was Brian. He walked across the basement floor and retrieved the other chair, dragging it along until he reached me. He spun it around and straddled it, resting his arms on the back as if he were about to engage in the most casual of conversations. He was far too close for my liking. To be fair, being in the same state as him was too close.

"Well, well, Kirsten O'Leary," he began, tapping his fingers on the metal frame as he spoke, "going by the fact that you didn't recognize my name, I'd take a guess you don't know who I am."

I considered not replying, but that wouldn't get me anywhere. "I recognize you from the vet clinic's CCTV footage. Should I know you?"

Brian gave me a dark look. "Of course your father never told you about me. That's just his style—gloss over anything that happened he'd rather forget. Well, Kirsten, I'm the man your mother was supposed to marry, before Liam 'Lucky' O'Leary stole her away."

"I'm supposed to believe that? After you kidnapped me at gunpoint and shot my friend, I'm supposed to believe anything you say?"

"I can understand your reluctance—obviously, you inherited your father's stubbornness, as well as his eyes, but it's the truth. Jane was my high school sweetheart, and in our senior year your father beat me half to death out of jealousy and forced Jane to be with him instead. How could she say no?

Your father had the entire Irish mob behind him. I'm sure she was terrified of the guy. Anybody would be. I couldn't blame her. I blamed him."

Brian's eyes were crazy, but it didn't seem like he was lying. Maybe, to him, it was the truth. I wasn't convinced.

Suddenly, he reached his hand out for my face. I recoiled but not quickly enough. He grabbed hold of my chin and forced me to lock eyes with him.

"What has this got to do with me?" I asked through clenched teeth. "Who gives a damn who liked who thirty years ago?"

Brian laughed. It was a horrific, ugly sound. "You know, other than your eyes, you're the spitting image of your mother. It's hard for me to look at you. Especially after the bitch put that restraining order out on me—as if I was going to let that stop me. She was mine."

A creeping shiver went up my spine. This was bad. Brian Feldman was insane. And there was no way to predict what a crazy person might do.

I forced myself to maintain conversation even as he leered at me. "If—if a restraining order wouldn't stop you, then what did you do?"

"Oh, wouldn't you like to know?" He laughed, a disturbing glint in his eyes that told me to prepare for the worst. "You should have been the product of it. I thought you were mine. For years and years when I was in prison, I dreamed of meeting my daughter, and then I saw you—took one look at you and knew. Those damn eyes. You were never mine. You were Liam's. All the hope I'd been clinging to was shattered once again by that bastard you call your father."

He continued on as if I weren't there. "So, I'd set myself up to take him down—get you thrown in jail so you could live through just a taste of what your parents did to me. And it was such a convenient guise under which the Russian mob could try to take down Liam. Or that leader of theirs they don't like. To be honest, I didn't care for that side of the plan, but I needed their manpower to pull all this off, and someone owed me a favor, so there you go. It worked like a charm. I knew the best way for me to get revenge against Liam O'Leary was to take someone he loves."

He paused, tilting my head from side to side as he regarded me. I didn't know what he was looking for or if he was looking for anything at all. Maybe he was waiting for me to speak.

I didn't.

"And so…here we are, Kirsten."

What was I supposed to say? I felt like I couldn't speak. This man—this monster—had attacked my mother, around the time she became pregnant with me. What if the trauma and stress from that had affected her pregnancy? What if—what if what Brian had done to my mother had indirectly killed her?

Suddenly, I was full of unfathomable rage, enough to overwrite the fear I'd been feeling.

I wrenched my face away from his hand, biting down hard when he tried to grab on to me again.

"You sick son of a bitch," I spat out as he furiously wiped

blood away from the side of his hand. I was happy to see I'd broken the skin.

"Funny," he growled, "that's what your mother said to me before I made love to her."

I reached out my hand to slap him, but he caught hold of my wrist and squeezed it in his iron grip. I couldn't help gasping in pain—the man was strong. When I saw his eyes roving over my dress, a fear that had nothing to do with whether I might die tonight came over me.

He wanted something else.

And with my sprained ankle, and a locked door, and armed guards on the other side, there was nowhere for me to go. I couldn't escape from the sociopath right in front of my eyes.

"You know, maybe it isn't fair to send you to prison, Kirsten. You didn't do anything wrong, after all," Brian said as he stood up, keeping hold of my wrist as he rose. He loomed over me, using his height against me. "But if you don't go to prison, I'll have to find another way to exact my revenge on your father."

I tried to back my chair away, but he caught the edge of the frame with his other hand. He ran his lips over the back of my wrist as he sneered at me.

My blood felt like it was made of ice.

"I think I know exactly how."

CHAPTER TWENTY-FOUR

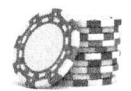

I was all frayed nerves, fear, and adrenaline when we finally reached the warehouse. There were two cars outside, which seemed to match up to Sergei's assumption that this was the right place. The lights were on—another good sign.

That also meant the building and its perimeter were likely teeming with armed Russian mob members. When the car Matt, Katya, Sergei, and Patrick were in drove beside Detective Peters' car, Matt rolled down the window to talk to us.

"That's a lot of guns to get through."

"I don't think there's going to be anything legal about getting through them all," I murmured in reply. Charles threw me a look.

"We're waiting for back-up. I've sent word we need it. It should be here in ten minutes."

I resisted the urge to scream at the man. Looking at Ian, he clearly suffered through the same urge.

"Charles, we can't—I don't think we have ten minutes to wait." I turned to look at Liam, whose mouth was set in a grim but determined line. "From what you told me about Feldman, the guy is a complete psycho. We can't possibly give him ten minutes."

Liam shook his head. "I'm not sparing even a second." He looked over at Sergei who was in the other car with his phone to his ear. "Are your men in position?"

Sergei nodded.

"Just so long as you don't catch them, right?" I threw back at Charles. He held his head in his hands.

"If this doesn't work, then never mind early retirement—I'll be fired." But then he sighed. "Do it. Feldman's case file gives me reason to agree with you. We don't have five minutes."

We watched from our cars as the sounds of gunfire filled the air. There was yelling and cursing and other sounds of alarm. After a few minutes of deafening noise, there was silence. When I attempted to get out of the car, Sergei held up his hand.

"Wait a minute. Let my men clear away the traitors."

Charles spluttered in disbelief. "You can't just take them all away."

"I can. Besides, my men didn't kill any of them if they could avoid it…merely wounded them. I have some questions I want answered." He almost laughed at the look on Charles' face. "You have eyewitnesses who could I.D. some guys from Ringo's, right?"

He nodded.

"Then when I'm done with them, I'll send them your way. With your eyewitness accounts, you'll be able to put them away for good. Does that work for you?"

Charles seemed to be struggling internally, but then he nodded. "Fine. It's the best deal I could hope to get from you people."

Sergei grinned humorlessly. "Then I'd say it's time to go in and steal back Miss Irish."

True to his word, the warehouse was eerily empty of the Russian mob and Sergei's men. I couldn't help wondering about how they'd escaped. All that was left were smears of blood here and there, a testament to the short yet brutal fight that had taken place while we sat in our cars outside.

Therein lay our problem. The warehouse was empty. Kirsten and Feldman were nowhere to be seen.

"Sergei, you were sure Feldman would still be with the mob," Katya cried out in despair. Despite all of us having tried to convince her to stay at Capone's, or at least to stay in the car, the woman had point-blank refused. I guess we'd all forgotten she'd been just as much a part of the violent, bloody life surrounding us as we all were.

Sergei fired her a look. "I still don't think I'm wrong. Search the warehouse and the area behind it thoroughly."

Charles and I went in one direction, a still silent Ian with his brother Patrick in another. Both Liam and Sergei paired up to check outside—an odd sight I never thought I'd get over. Matt and Katya investigated the front of the warehouse.

After ten minutes of searching, there was nothing to be found.

Ian caught my eye from the other side of the warehouse. At this distance, I could see he was distraught. What could we do?

Where was Kirsten? If she wasn't in the warehouse, then where was she?

"Volkov, she isn't here," Liam O'Leary bit out. I could tell he'd been trying to keep it together for his family's sake, but he was unraveling before me with every passing moment.

This was his baby girl—the last remnant of the life he had with his beloved wife. Had he been granted a new daughter in Katya, only to have Kirsten ripped away from him?

It wasn't something I wanted to dwell on.

Sergei didn't respond, but he pulled out his cell phone and spoke to someone, angrily, in Russian. When finally he hung up, he looked confused.

"She's here with that Feldman guy. My men got one of the traitors to talk. They definitely came here."

"So where are they?" both Patrick and Matt exclaimed in exasperation.

"There's no way he escaped with her," Katya said in a small voice. "How did your men get away without us seeing them, Sergei?"

"Around the back. There's another door, but my men said there were no tracks—human, car, or otherwise. They had men guarding the back door the whole time they were here. This Feldman guy couldn't have possibly escaped that way with Kirsten."

Ian punched a television box that sat upon a stray pallet in frustration. The stack of boxes moved forward on its wheels just a few inches.

"Shit! Shit…"

Ian's curses became muted in my head as I stared at the pallets. There were six of them in total. Four were against the wall, but two of them stood a few feet in front of the others.

"Ian," I murmured, then yelled, "Ian!"

I pushed away one of the pallets. Ian caught on to what I was doing and pushed the other one away.

There beneath our feet was a door. I put my ear against it and could barely hear the sound of movement. With shaking hands, I tried to open it, but it was sealed shut with a lock.

Everyone surrounded me, Ian, and the door at this point. "It's locked," I said simply. "We need something—anything—to open it."

Katya rushed to my side, dropping to her knees with a knife in her hand. I looked at her, and she raised an eyebrow.

"Why do you all keep forgetting how I was brought up? I've got this."

Katya worked on the lock with deft hands, making quick work of the mechanism with her knife until it clicked open.

I wasted no time hauling the thick, heavy door open. As soon as it was open, I heard Kirsten's muffled cries clear as day.

"Kirsten!" I screamed as I vaulted down the stairs. I was blind with rage and fear, barely conscious of the fact that Ian and his father and brother followed closely behind me.

I saw her. I saw my Kirsten, bloody and bruised, desperately trying to push Feldman away as he held a hand over her mouth. There were tears streaming down her face, but she'd given as good as she got. Feldman's arms were covered in bleeding, weeping scratch marks.

I threw myself at the man as soon I locked eyes with him, throwing him off Kirsten in seconds. My fist connected with the side of his face, again and again and again. The man was too shocked to respond. I was too strong. Too determined. Too damn angry.

I wanted to kill him, law be damned. I was going to kill him.

Instead, Ian pulled me off the asshole.

"Let him rot in prison, Rafe."

I stared at him, not quite believing what I heard. "You punch me in the face for sneaking out your sister's window, but you're against me beating the shit out of this psychopath?"

"I don't want you to go to prison for murdering his scum ass, that's all. It's not worth it." And then, as if proving a point, he picked up the barely conscious Feldman by the collar of his shirt and swiftly punched him in the face. "See? I have nothing against merely beating him up."

"Unfortunately, I do," Charles interjected, moving Ian out of the way to cuff Feldman. As he read the man his rights, I swung my head around to look at Kirsten.

She hadn't moved from her position on the floor, clearly in shock.

"Rafe?" she croaked out. She just barely moved her eyes to take in the rest of the people in the basement. "You all...found me."

I collapsed by her side, pulling her into my arms and keeping her pressed against my chest.

"We did...of course, we did. Can't believe you ever doubted us."

She glanced past me. "Da?"

Liam got down on his knees by my side, stroking Kirsten's hair away from her face as he smiled at her, tears streaming down his face. "I'm here, love. I'm sorry. I'm so sorry."

"You've got some 'splaining to do," Kirsten mumbled as she passed out against my chest.

"We need to get her to a hospital," Ian said.

Patrick already had his phone in his hand. He moved like lightning up the stairs to make the call. In the distance, I could barely hear police sirens.

If we had waited for Charles' backup, we really would have been too late. I didn't want to think about what might have happened had we found Kirsten any later than we did.

"What the hell?" a garbled voice said. It was Brian, barely conscious and struggling to speak through the mess I'd made of his face. "Lucky O'Leary working with the head of the Russian mob. What the—hell?"

"You underestimate what I'll do for my family," Liam replied coldly. His fists were clenched and shaking. I had no doubt he wanted to murder the asshole who'd dared to lay a hand on both his wife and daughter even more than I did. "Though I'm surprised you didn't know that, given what happened last time."

"So long as I'm alive, you haven't won."

Liam's icy silence spoke volumes.

Feldman wasn't worth his time. He was done. The man no longer existed. If I knew Lucky O'Leary, Feldman's days were numbered.

Several policemen appeared and took Feldman out of the basement first. I carried Kirsten out, followed by her family and Sergei.

"You helped me stamp out the traitors who wanted me out, and I helped you find your daughter, so we're even, O'Leary," I heard Sergei murmur to Liam as the ambulance arrived.

"What you did for me was more than I did for you, Volkov. Consider me owing you a favor in thanks."

I could tell Sergei was grinning without seeing it. "I'll hold you to that." There was no doubt he would. Debts were always paid.

Only one of us was allowed to sit in the ambulance with Kirsten. I stood aside to let her father climb in, but he shook his head.

"You go, Rafe. We wouldn't have known what was going on as quickly as we did if it weren't for you."

If it weren't for Dean, you mean, I thought humbly, angry beyond measure at myself, but I nodded my head.

"I'll see you all at the hospital."

As I sat beside an unconscious Kirsten, I finally had time to look at her thoroughly. Half of the wounds on her were clearly the result of her having fought like the scrappy, reckless idiot she was. God, I'd never loved that part of her as much as I did now. It was likely the only thing that had kept Feldman at bay long enough for us to find her in time.

God, I loved her so much. I wasn't going to waste any more of my life—or hers—finding reasons not to tell her that.

I'd tell her every day. I'd tell her every hour.

I loved Kirsten O'Leary, and nothing was going to stop me from loving her forever.

I just had to make sure I used a door to visit her from now on.

CHAPTER TWENTY-FIVE

I slept for almost three full days. It wasn't the kind of sleep that felt like any time had passed while I was unconscious. It didn't feel as though I'd only been asleep momentarily either. I didn't know how to explain it. I'd expected to feel disoriented, foggy and confused after waking up from so much sleep, but instead, I felt refreshed and renewed.

Well…except for the tender bruises and stinging cuts slowly healing across my body, and the ache of my severely sprained ankle.

With the pain came all the memories associated with it. I shivered in my hospital bed despite myself, but my father was sitting there watching me, and his eyes lit up when he saw me awake. He cried as he held my hand and felt me shake and then called for the doctor, who took my vitals, had a nurse bring me food and water, then gave me a low dose of a sedative to help calm my nerves.

When the shaking subsided, my father sat by my head and stroked my hair.

"I am so sorry, my baby girl."

"You don't have anything to be sorry for, Da," I half-croaked, my voice hoarse from disuse. I gulped down some water, coughed a little, then repeated the sentiment.

My father sighed. "I have everything to be sorry for."

"Really, what were you supposed to do about a Russian mob coup and a psychopath?"

"I could have killed the man after he attacked your mother. I should have killed him before he attacked your mother, and then maybe…"

"Da, don't you dare say any of those things," I said firmly, though a tight lump in my throat threatened tears. "That's not who you are. If you had killed him, then you might not be here, and you definitely wouldn't be the man I'm proud to call my Da."

He was silent. Clearly, he didn't know what to say.

"Just tell me one thing."

"What, my love?"

"Tell me the full story. Tell me everything about this—this Feldman guy, and how he knew Mom. Tell me the real story of how you ended up together. I somehow doubt the warped version I got from him is the truth."

My father's face darkened at the mere thought of Feldman

having given me an account of what happened, but then the darkness was gone and he smiled sadly.

"Of course, Kirsten. I should have told you long ago."

The story was tough to hear, and awful—terrible, so terrible—but I smiled along with my father when he told me about how he'd protected my mother with no ulterior motive whatsoever. How his 'fake' relationship with her had blossomed into something genuine, and how this resulted in them marrying straight out of high school, so completely and utterly in love with each other.

Despite the awful things that had happened, we both laughed and cried bittersweet tears by the end of my father's explanation.

"Why did you never tell me any of this before?" I asked. "I could have…I could have handled it, especially since it finally explained how the two of you got together."

My father stared out of the window of my hospital room, his eyes a little distant.

"I was afraid. You didn't know, so I didn't need to see the sadness in your eyes whenever you thought about it. I saw it in Patrick and Ian's eyes sometimes, and each time it was like a knife had been thrust into my heart. You already had your mother's death looming over you—who was I to give you more to be sad about concerning her?"

I understood it, I really did, and yet still I wished I had known. Then it suddenly occurred to me.

"Rafe knew, didn't he?"

"Only recently. Only after the break-in of your apartment.

I saw the theft of your photo for what it was, and I would have been a fool not to inform the man defending you."

"That explains…so much."

"Please don't blame him for not telling you, Kirsten," my dad implored. "Your brothers and I weren't exactly friendly when we told him not to tell you. Rafe will have felt like it was not his place to tell you about matters that concerned the O'Leary family."

I sighed. "I know. I get it. He's too honorable."

"Not so honorable as to resist the urge to sneak in through your window, it seems."

I threw a pillow at my father's face. "Not fair. Had I been allowed to stay in my apartment, he'd have never had to do it."

He laughed. "Just so long as he uses a door next time, I don't care."

That's how Rafe found us, laughing and making jibes at each other as if nothing terrible whatsoever had happened over the past few weeks.

He rushed to my side, embracing me despite my father being present. "You're awake," he mumbled into my hair. "You're awake. Thank God."

I pulled away slightly to kiss him. "As if you were going to get rid of me that easily."

Rafe let out a garbled noise, halfway between a cry and a laugh. "Only you could joke about this so easily."

And then I remembered something that decidedly couldn't be joked about and my face grew pale. "Rafe. Is Dean…"

"He's fine, Kirsten," he soothed, smiling warmly down at me. "Well, as fine as a man who was shot twice can be. Luckily, neither bullet hit any major organs—a miracle, really. He's recovering well if you want to go and see him."

"Yes. Now," I said, getting up immediately, though I swayed a little in doing so. Both Rafe and my father helped me stay upright.

"Are you sure that's a good idea, my love?" my father asked. "Maybe get some more rest first."

I stared at him levelly. "If it weren't for Dean, you wouldn't have known what was going on so quickly," I said, though nobody had told me whether he'd ever managed to tip Rafe off. Given how quickly everyone found me, and the look on Rafe's face confirming my suspicions, there was no doubt in my mind what Dean had done. "He took two bullets for me. I can take a little light-headedness in order to thank him."

My father seemed thoroughly proud by my decision. "Then I'll come with you. It seems I have just as much reason to thank the man, if not more."

So my father came with me to Dean's room, Rafe taking me by the hand and showing us both the way. When we reached the room, a young, attractive nurse was flirting outrageously with Dean, who was politely chuckling along with whatever joke the nurse said.

As soon as Dean saw me and his eyes lit up with genuine delight, it suddenly became clear to me just how superficial the charm was he used as armor against getting close to anyone else the whole time I'd known him. I decided I would force him to rectify that. He'd said himself he would get over me. It was only fair he gave other women a real chance to get to know him.

"O'Leary, you look awful," Dean joked as I sat down on his bed, tears in my eyes. Dean looked haggard and pale though just a little color returned to his cheeks when he saw me.

"You look pretty shitty yourself, Boss. How are the bullet holes?"

"Feeling very much like bullet holes, but I'll live. Is this your father?" he asked, glancing over my shoulder.

My father stepped forward and shook Dean's hand as I moved out of the way. "I hear I owe you an immeasurable debt."

"I don't suppose Kirsten can pay it off by working for me for free?"

"Shut up, Dean," I cut in, rolling my eyes.

He laughed and then grew serious. "There is no debt, Mr. O'Leary. I did what I did of my own choosing. I'd do it again. You can plainly see your daughter means a lot to me."

My father glanced at Dean and then at Rafe.

"Rafe, I never knew you had such intimidating competition."

Dean winced. "Ah, no, he doesn't. Kirsten turned me down flat. The broken heart hurts more than the bullet holes."

"Shut up, Dean," I repeated, though I was laughing.

"In all honesty," Dean continued, "I was never truly in the

race, but that's okay. I only hope not to lose Kirsten as a friend and colleague. She's indispensable to the clinic."

"You know I'm not going nowhere," I replied, smiling. Out of the corner of my eye, I noticed Rafe freeze a little, so I gave his hand a squeeze before reaching over and hugging Dean. "I need to talk to Rafe, but I'll see you later."

"I'll hold you to that."

When we reached my hospital room once more, my father excused himself to call my brothers and let them know I'd woken up.

Rafe sat down on the chair a few feet from my bed. He looked at me with doubt and uncertainty in his eyes.

"What's wrong?" I asked, worried and confused.

"I'm so sorry, Kirsten."

"You sound like my father. I'm done with the apologies."

"I should have told you everything."

"Yeah, you should have, but you didn't. I understand why, so it's okay. I'm—okay. I think. So stop being sorry."

"If you don't want to be with me after all of this, I—"

"Okay, stop right there," I interrupted, finally understanding why he was looking at me the way he was. "Are you breaking up with me?"

Rafe stared at me, surprised. "You said you were going to stay in Vegas and work at the Collins Vet Clinic."

"And?"

"So you…don't want to leave anymore?"

"Why should that have anything to do with me and you? When I wanted to run, I wanted to run from my problems. But they're sorted out. There's no barrier for us to be together now. Rafe—I love you. I love you so much, but I love my job too, and despite it all, I love this city. I don't want to leave if I really don't have to."

Relief washed over Rafe's face. "Would you still want to be with me if I weren't a lawyer?"

I blinked at him, nonplussed. "Huh?"

"I just—I realized with this case, I don't want to defend bastards like Feldman. It's not so far-flung an idea to think I'll have more than a few clients just like him. I don't think I have it in me to set them free. Your case was hard enough, and you were completely innocent. Not to mention the person I love most in the world."

I blushed at the sentiment, then smiled. "Rafe, you could be an unemployed lazy ass for all I care. You certainly have the family money for it. I just want you to be happy. Can you be happy staying in Vegas with me?"

Rafe left the chair to sit by my side on the bed. He took my hands in his.

"It's all I've ever wanted."

"Then maybe we should start looking at alternative career options for you."

"I thought you said I could be a lazy ass?"

"I changed my mind. That would be awful."

"What a cruel woman."

I laughed. Rafe gently kissed me, and I happily reciprocated.

"I love you, Rafe."

"I love you, too."

Despite the pain in my ankle, and despite the memories of the past few weeks still sitting fresh in my mind, I felt a wave of excitement wash over me.

Maybe my life with Rafe Wilde could really begin.

After all, it was all I'd ever wanted.

CHAPTER TWENTY-SIX

"So Gemma said she *really* liked you."

"Ah, she was too...uptight."

"Dean, you said the same thing about Emma last week."

"Well—she was."

"Meredith was too laid back?"

"Exactly."

"Dean," I sighed, taking a swig of coffee as I did so, "your standards are impossible. How did you ever fall for Kirsten in the first place? It doesn't seem like she'd have made the cut."

"Rude," Kirsten called over from the coffee maker in the kitchen of the Collins Vet Clinic. I was sitting at the table with Dean, having brought along the lunch Kirsten had forgotten.

I had quit the law firm, and it was as if a huge weight had been lifted from my shoulders. I had celebrated the feeling of finally having a break—an easy, stress-free break I'd filled with matchmaking for Dean.

After everything that had happened, I'd discovered to my surprise the two of us actually got along. It was a friendship that had come straight out of left field, and Kirsten still hadn't gotten used to it.

Let's face it—I needed some new friends. After the stress and long hours of my law-oriented life, the only genuine friend I seemed to have left was Ian. We were back on good terms. Being unemployed made me realize just how much I'd relied on the man for social company.

I had a lot to fix about my life, so I'd started with making a new friend. So much for not bothering Kirsten at work because I had nothing else to do.

Well, that wasn't exactly true. The story of Jane O'Leary, as well as what had happened to Kirsten, shed new light on what I could do with my law degree. I'd been providing law advice at the local woman's shelter for free, to the point where I attracted a job offer to do exactly what I was doing but actually get paid. It didn't pay much, but I didn't need much. I had Kirsten, and she was enough

I intended to take them up on it soon. Just not right now.

In a month or two, maybe. For now, I was enjoying taking some time for myself and Kirsten, taking her to the movies or to the casino or simply staying in, bingeing television shows and cooking her dinner—something I never found time to do for myself, let alone for anyone else. Turned out I was great at it, and Kirsten delighted in getting to eat good food without eating out all the time.

Dean groaned. "Not that I don't appreciate the effort you're putting into this, Rafe, but maybe give me a week or two without dates. This old man is exhausted."

"Dean, you're thirty-nine next week, not seventy," Kirsten interjected as she sat down beside us, tearing hungrily into her sandwich when I handed it to her.

"You used to enjoy telling me I was old."

"That was before you nearly died. I think that requires some niceness from me."

"How magnanimous of you. Well, in return, I can be nice too. Take the afternoon off."

Kirsten stared at Dean. "You're willingly giving me a free afternoon?"

Dean glanced at me. "Just take him with you. Go do something, *anything,* to keep him from setting me up with another girl he knew from college."

Kirsten laughed as I spluttered in indignation, getting up from her seat to grab her denim jacket from the coatroom attached to the kitchen. "You don't need to tell me twice I have a free afternoon. Come on, Rafe. Let's head back to my place."

The eyebrow Kirsten raised told me all I needed to know. We were out of the clinic in under ten seconds as Dean chuckled behind us.

I had a better idea than going back to Kirsten's apartment. I'd picked her up in the Audi Quattro, having grown attached to the car. She looked at me, confused, as I drove in the completely wrong direction.

"Where are we going, Rafe?" she asked.

"You'll see."

When we reached the city limits, Kirsten frowned.

"You're not kidnapping me, are you?"

"Hardly. I just thought—maybe—we could live out part of the fantasy of running away? Just for an afternoon."

"Well…what did you have in mind?"

I glanced pointedly at a hotel up ahead.

"That's the first hotel out of the city limits. That was the extent of my plans."

Kirsten grinned. "Sounds good to me."

We checked into the hotel in a hurry, the two of us hardly able to keep our hands off each other.

When we reached the room, I barely gave Kirsten an opportunity to take off her jacket before I picked her up in my arms and carried her over to the bed, kissing her passionately as I did so.

She happily reciprocated, giggling as the two of us dropped onto the bed.

"You know, if we keep doing it at the rate we're going, eventually you'll be too exhausted to," I joked as I unbuttoned her blouse and peeled it off her skin before undressing myself.

"Hardly. We're making up for lost time. A lot of lost time."

"I guess I could be okay with that."

I didn't think I'd ever get sick of seeing Kirsten in nothing but her underwear, yet I wanted her naked even more. It was all I could do to discard her bra before Kirsten pulled me back to her once more, crushing my lips against hers as her hands roamed freely across my skin.

Kirsten's fingers pressed more insistently into my back as I kissed the hollow of her neck, following the line of her collarbone before gently nibbling on her left shoulder. She moaned. "Stop teasing me, Rafe…"

She brought my mouth back to hers with a demanding hand through my hair, then I gave in to my desire for the woman below me. When I entered her, she gasped in pleasure, then kissed me all the more passionately. The slow give and take of our lovemaking pulled sounds of pleasure from her I'd never tire of hearing. Our bodies were as perfectly matched as our souls.

Just like the first time we'd finally fallen into each other's arms, we didn't stop for a long time. It was only when a different kind of hunger took hold of me that Kirsten and I finally broke away from each other.

"Room service?" I suggested.

She laughed rather breathlessly. "What, no home cooking today?"

"I'd be somewhat impressed if I was able to cook inside a hotel room."

"Fair point. Burgers, fries, and shakes?"

"Change the shakes out for beer, and you have yourself a deal."

"Done," she replied, picking up the phone by the bedside to order for us.

Then I pulled her back against my side, kissing along her spine as my arms wrapped around her waist.

"Think we have time for one more round before the food arrives?" I murmured into Kirsten's ear. I was satisfied to feel her face heat back up.

"If the shower is big enough for two, then why not?"

Oh, I liked the sound of that. We could clean ourselves off and defile each other simultaneously. Ever the practical woman was Kirsten O'Leary.

"I love you," I said as Kirsten captured my mouth once more.

"You, too, Rafe Wilde."

We never made it to the shower.

CHAPTER TWENTY-SEVEN

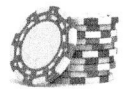

I peeked into the chapel to find all the usual suspects. Funny to see the pews integrated with members from all mob factions. There were no sections for the Italians, the Irish, or the Russians. Even the Columbians were interspersed. Off to the side was Detective Peters, who sat with Faye's FBI father. Never in my life would I have imagined a wedding like this. It was like housing cats and dogs in the same cage. It was doable but dangerous.

"You're not supposed to be out here. What if Rafe sees you?" Katya looked in all directions before she pulled me back into the dressing room.

"If Rafe sees me, I can guarantee we'll be late to our own wedding. That man has quite the sexual appetite."

Katya smiled. "All the Wilde men are animals in the bedroom."

Faye walked up to place my veil on my head. "Amen to that." She'd just found out they were expecting their first child.

"It's a good thing I specialize in animals." I turned to look at myself in the mirror. A tear ran down my cheek. It was part joy and part sadness. My mother should have been here on this day. And while I felt her physical absence, I also felt her spiritual presence. I'd taken her wedding photo to Faye and Katya's bridal shop and had a similar gown custom made. On my head was my mother's original veil, placed in storage for my wedding. As I stared at myself in the mirror, I saw how like her I was.

The stories everyone told were of a strong woman who loved fiercely. She was dedicated to her job and devoted to her family. I was told she had a wicked sense of humor that was tempered by her sweet side. I was still working on my sweet side.

"You look beautiful," Faye said as she wiped the tear from her face.

"She's passable," Katya added with a smile on her face. She turned me around and looked at my ass. I waited for her to make a remark. She'd once told Faye she looked like Snow White but maybe she shouldn't have eaten the seven dwarfs in one sitting. She was also self-deprecating when she claimed her own ass looked like two crackers in a paper sack. No one was off-limits to Katya, and I loved her for her boldness.

"Go ahead and say it." We'd been practicing disparaging sisterly comments for weeks. Lord knows we had so much time to make up for. I had over two decades of torture to give her just to catch up. She was an overachiever and beat me to the punch line every time.

"Say what?" Katya asked innocently, but behind those blue eyes was a tigress waiting to strike. In truth, she was a kitten that hid behind the tough Russian persona she grew up with and hadn't been able to shake. I loved her anyway.

"Whatever mean thing you're going to say about my ass."

"I was only going to say one day big butts will be in style and you can tell everyone you've had yours forever." She leaned in and kissed my cheek. "But really, you look fabulous."

I waited for the but that didn't come.

"That's all you got?"

She laughed. "I'm working on it. I've already used my good stuff on Faye."

Faye stepped back and smiled. "Don't listen to her. You're beautiful, and you're ready."

I was ready. I'd been in love with Rafe Wilde all my life. While I hadn't planned on racing to the altar, my father was Irish and old-fashioned. Ever since he learned of Rafe sneaking in my window, he'd been dropping hints about marriage.

The door swung open, and Rose raced inside. "Sorry I'm late. You know Josh? Well, he—" Her blush said it all. I stared at my bridesmaids. How lucky had I gotten with my upcoming marriage? Not only did I get two more Wilde brothers to call family, I got another sister in Faye. Since Josh had moved to Las Vegas, I was able to keep Rose as a good friend.

My father walked in and gasped. "You look beautiful," he said in Gaelic. It was a language he only used on special occasions—when he had something profound and emotional to say, or when I was about to get my ass beat for some infraction. Today, his words were beautiful.

"Are you ready?"

"I've been ready to marry Rafe since I was born."

My dad offered me his arm. "I've always known you had a love for the wild side. Never thought you'd marry one, but I think you chose well. He's a good man, and he knows I'll kill him if he ever makes you cry."

I kissed my father on the cheek as we all lined up and waited for the music to play.

"You won't have to kill him, Da. I can neuter him while he sleeps."

My father chuckled. "That's my girl."

Alex, Matt, and Dean escorted Faye, Katya, and Rose to the front of the church, respectively. I never had to watch where I stepped. I kept my eyes on Rafe, and my heart led me to him.

"I love you," he whispered as he took me from my father and walked me to the altar.

"I love you too."

Who would have ever thought the Wildes, Petrenkos, and O'Learys would bind themselves together for life? There were bound to be disputes, but we all agreed to check our weapons and bring our hearts to the table if we ever found ourselves at odds with one another.

The priest performed the ceremony and ended it with an Irish blessing.

May the road rise up to meet you.

May the wind always be at your back.

May the sun shine warm upon your face,

And rains fall soft upon your fields.

And until we meet again,

May God hold you in the palm of His hand.

Father O'Connor looked out at the attendees before he leaned forward and whispered, "And may you leave quickly before all hell breaks loose."

We walked down the aisle and out the front door toward our new lives together. This was going to be some kind of Wilde love.

A SNEAK PEEK AT REDEEMING RYKER
RYKER-TWENTY YEARS AGO

Chapter One

Raptor Savage didn't put up with losers. He didn't put up with laziness, and he didn't put up with liars. Today, I was all three.

The sunbaked asphalt pulled at my sneakers. The trees whispered, *'turn around, run for your life.'* Each inchworm step I took closer to home slapped my backpack against my butt, but that was nothing compared to the ass whoopin' I'd get from Dad today.

My report on Abraham Lincoln had been due today, the same report I'd told my mom I'd finished, which meant I was a liar. I hadn't done the stupid report. Hiding out in the shop, and listening to the War Birds talk strategy, was more fun than writing about a dead president. That made me a lazy loser. I'd gotten a big fat zero for my grade.

Dad would shout, *the report is important, school, and getting educated is the only job you have.* And I'd roll my eyes or shake my head or just let my shoulder's slump. Abraham Lincoln couldn't teach me a thing. He was dead.

Ask me to write about the gun that killed him, and I would have brought home an easy A. Guns, I knew.

I snaked through the bikes lined up like dominoes in the gravel parking lot as my backpack slipped from my shoulders.

So many bikes at the club meant trouble. Dad was busy, so maybe I wouldn't get a butt blistering after all.

As the president of the War Birds MC, this was Dad's world, and Mom said he ran it like he was God.

God made the laws. He made the rules. He handed down the punishments. Raptor Savage could make people shake in their sneakers with the lift of an eyebrow. I got that look a lot.

Mom always said my spirited nature would serve me well when I grew up and took over the club. Dad always put an "if" before that statement. "If he grows up."

I stepped back from the door and slipped around the side of the building. Mom was out back with my brothers, Silas and Decker. Next to them was that pesky little girl, Sparrow. She always looked up at me like I was a movie star.

"Glad you're home, sweetie." Mom never called me sweetie in front of anyone else because that would make me seem like a sissy, but I liked when she said it. "Today's Dad's big meeting, so I need you to hang out here with the kids. I have to get inside and serve beer."

I looked around the parking lot at the motorcycles I didn't recognize. "Who's here?"

"Friends of your father's. It has nothing to do with you."

I glared at the kids playing in the dirt. "That's not true." My voice didn't sound like eight-year-old me. It sounded more like six-year-old Silas when Mom told him to take a bath. "I have to babysit, and that means it has everything to do with me." I hated babysitting. Silas was fine. At six, he took care of himself. But Decker was just a baby, which meant diapers, and then there was Sparrow. She stuck to me like gum on a shoe.

I threw my backpack toward the stairs. It skidded across the gravel and clunked to a stop against the bottom step. "Is this about Goose?" Goose was a War Bird who'd been killed last week after a cop stopped him for speeding. I didn't understand it—Goose was a good guy.

Mom looked over her shoulder toward the club entrance. "Not now, Ryker."

Uh oh. She'd called me Ryker, which meant she was losing her patience. I looked toward the kids and let out a long breath. "Okay, but is this about the cop who shot Goose?" Officer Stuart had said Goose pulled a gun first, but that had to be a big, fat lie. Goose would never shoot the police. Dad's words replayed through my head: *'That cop has been targeting motorcycle gangs. His goal is to clean up Fury.'* Fury was a small dot in the mountains. The entire town couldn't fill up the high school sports stadium. How much cleaning up did we need?

"Dad invited the Rebels over to discuss the growing

tension in the area. He needs to get it under control before more people get hurt. I need you to help me out." Mom put her fingers under my chin and closed my open mouth. "Take good care of them." She didn't wait but walked in to the club. The club that would someday be mine.

"Hi, Hawk," Using my nickname, Sparrow pulled on my hand. Her fingers were pink and sticky. "Want some candy?" She reached into the pocket of her dress and pulled out a piece of lint-covered licorice.

"Gross." I yanked the candy from her little fist and tossed it toward the parking lot. "It's dirty."

"It's mine." She took off toward the candy that lay in the dirt.

With two giant steps, I grabbed her around her waist, swiping her off the ground.

The rumble of motorcycle engines stopped me like I'd walked into a brick wall. Pulling in front of the club were at least ten more Rebels. "Too many."

I raced back to the playpen where Decker slept. Silas drew in the dirt with a stick, and I dropped Sparrow to her sandaled feet.

"Silas, watch them for a minute." I'd never seen the Rebels up close, and I didn't want to miss my chance.

He looked up at me with Dad's eyes. Steel, gray eyes that said it all even before the words came out. "You're supposed to stay with us."

Sparrow stomped her little feet, causing the soles of her shoes to light up. "Yeah." She looked up at me with the crazy cool eyes only she had. "You're supposed to sit with me." Her one blue, and one brown, eyes begged me to stay.

"I'll be right back. Stay here." I crept to the corner of the club and wiggled the loose board just enough to slip inside the storage room. The place smelled like leather and sweat and anger, but I tiptoed forward and slid behind the stack of crates. I pressed my ear to the crack between the boxes.

Dad's voice was loud and clear and calm. He talked about rival gangs, feuds, the sheriff, and what they were going to do.

I peeked over the crate of brake pads and counted the heads I didn't recognize. There were twenty-five Rebels in our nest. This was epic. Never had there been so many enemies in one place without someone needing a doctor.

Something creaked behind me, and I swung around.

Sparrow squeezed through the hole. *Little brat.* "What are you doing?" I whispered. "Go back," I gritted through my teeth.

"No." She said, a little too loud.

I slapped my hand over her mouth. "Shh. This is a secret." I pulled her close. "You can stay if you can be quiet."

She nodded, and I went back to my hiding place. She tucked up next to me, and we listened. Or, really, I listened while she peeled the stickers from the boxes in front of us. At least she was being quiet.

All the War Birds were there. Well, all but Goose. Kite, Dad's vice president, screamed about being targeted. Some of the members paced the room. They reminded me of the time I cornered a stray cat in the garage. Its hair stood on its back while its tail twitched from side to side.

I'd once heard someone say, '*the tension was so thick you could cut it with a knife.*' I never understood what that meant until now. The air was thick like Mom's pudding, and it was hard to breathe.

"Your problems aren't my problems." The rebel leader leaned back and crossed his hulk-sized arms over his chest.

"It won't be long before it spreads to your club." Dad leaned forward with his elbows on his knees. "Can't we have a truce between the two clubs until the problem with the police is under control? We don't need to be fighting wars from every side."

Mom crossed in front of me with a full tray of bottled beer. I ducked lower so she wouldn't see me. Sparrow's mom, Finch, followed behind picking up the empties. I didn't know her real name. No one went by their real name at the club. We were War Birds with names like Hawk, Raptor, Kite, and Vulture. The women always chose stupid sissy birds like Warble, Robin, or Sparrow. I looked down at the little bird next to me. She wasn't so bad. She was like me —spirited.

The front door burst open and a pair of cops filled the doorway.

Dad jumped from his seat. "This is a private meeting," he pointed to the door, "and private property."

The big cop, the ugly one, put his hand on the butt of his gun. "Just here to keep the peace." There was something creepy about his voice. Something dangerous about the way his fingers scratched against the gun.

"Only peace here." Dad spread his arms wide enough to stretch open his leather jacket and show off his War Bird belt buckle. The belt usually held his gun, but he carried no gun today. He was in a room of enemies—unprotected. Or so it seemed. I knew Dad, and he no doubt had a plan.

Mom popped the tops off two beers and handed them to the cops.

To my surprise, they took them. I guess they didn't have to obey the rules. They were cops.

Finch passed in front of us, and Sparrow sprang to her feet. I knew she would bolt toward her mother, so I picked her up and tossed her backward toward the broken panel. She stumbled against one box, knocking it down. The loud bang shattered the silence.

Everything changed in an instant. Guns drew and shots fired—lots of shots. Bullets flew through the air with the hiss of a mosquito, only a thousand times louder. Metal hit metal with the ding of a pinball machine. Wood splintered from the rafters above.

People fell to the ground in front of me. Sparrow screamed and I grabbed her, crouching with her behind the brake boxes and prayed we wouldn't be next. Prayed until my mom crumpled to the ground. "Mom." Still holding Sparrow, I sprung from my hiding place and ran to where she lay in a pool of blood.

"Where are your brothers?" Her words, no more than a

whisper, were hard to hear with the popping sounds filling the air. I crushed Sparrow beneath me and hugged the cement floor.

"Outside. They're safe outside." I reached for Mom, trying to find her wound.

Sparrow popped her head from under me and screamed.

Mom's eyes grew wide. "Get her out. Save her. Save your brothers." Her words slipped slow and wet from her lips. "Promise."

The wooden beams splintered, sending chunks of wood flying through the air. Clouds of white chalk burst from the walls.

My heart exploded in my chest, and tears ran down my cheeks. "Mommy."

Her head fell to the side.

"Mommy." I was a man but cried like a child. "Don't leave me." I turned her face toward mine and wiped the blood that trickled from her mouth. "I promise."

Her once bright blue eyes faded to the color of cold, gray concrete.

Bullets buzzed. People collapsed. Sparrow screamed and screamed and screamed.

I swept her into my arms and ran toward the door, but hot fire shot through my shoulder. I stumbled. I fell. Blood covered the walls, the floor, the bodies.

I scrambled to stand, but my sneakers slid on the smooth concrete. I slipped and fell over and over again until I couldn't move. I couldn't breathe. I was going to die.

Sparrow lay beside me, but she was quiet. Dead quiet. Blood seeped across her yellow dress like spilled ink on paper. The bright sunflower pattern disappeared in the crimson pool.

I'd failed. I'd failed Sparrow. I'd failed my brothers. I'd failed to keep my mom's final wish. "I promise I'll never fail anyone again," I cried. Everything turned to black.

Chapter Two
Ana-Present Day

I walked inside The Wayfair Lounge, tugging at my clothes. This wasn't the place a girl went dressed in jeans and a ratty sweater, but I didn't care. I wasn't looking to hook up. I was looking for Grace.

Men in suits walked the edge of the bar, shopping the seated women like they were goods on a shelf. Waving like a lunatic in need of a white buckled jacket, Grace jumped from the corner booth. Her stilettos clicked on the wood floor, the gauzy fabric of her skirt swished around her legs.

Every man's gaze fell on those long limbs.

"You made it." She noosed my neck and pulled me in for a hug. "What do you want to drink?"

"Water." I slid into the booth and plopped my purse on top of the table.

"You can't drink water." Grace waved to the bartender, motioned to her Cosmo, and held up two fingers.

"I can't afford anything but water." I pulled my wallet from my purse and opened it to reveal a lone ten-dollar bill. It was the only money I had until next week when I'd get paid for my last design job—a flier for the new donut shop on Colfax. It wasn't the work I'd envisioned when I graduated with a graphics design degree, but it paid some of the bills.

"This one is on me." She looked me up and down, then frowned. "If you had dressed for the place, the drinks could have been on him." She nodded toward Mr. Pinstripe, leaning against the wall, and staring. Staring at Grace. I might as well have been invisible.

I grabbed Grace's glass, and the drink sloshed over the side. I sucked the sticky liquid that ran down my fingers.

"Keep doing that, and the whole bar will buy you drinks. It won't matter what you're wearing."

I popped my finger from my mouth. Yep, at least a dozen men zoned in on my mouth—my lips—my tongue. The heat of a blush rose to my cheeks.

The bartender set a tray of drinks on our table. He looked around the room and nodded toward several men. "Compliments of your admirers."

Grace pulled out a twenty and slid it in the bartender's pocket. "Thanks, Tony."

"No problem. Cosmos for the next round?" he asked, as if we'd just slammed the first round.

I shook my head. "No more for me." After two of these, I'd be done. Three would have me slurring my words. Four, and I'd be waking up some place strange with a hairy chest pressed to my face.

"Keep them coming and keep them the same." Grace gave him her Hollywood smile. "No one wants a sick date. You know the saying: Mix your liquor, never been sicker." She toasted her martini at the crowd. "Here's to man-whore Mondays."

The bartender laughed and left.

"I've got to stop coming here with you." It was the truth. The past several Mondays I'd tipped back a few too many martinis and made too many poor choices. Mondays never produced the right kind of men. I wanted more than an in-the-minute Mike. I wanted a long-term Luke. "I don't get it. I'm smart. I'm funny. I'm low maintenance. I'm not crazy. I can pull off sexy. Shouldn't I be beating men off with a stick?"

"With a stick?" Grace was half a martini to full-on giddy drunk. "In my experience, they'd prefer you beat them off with your hand." She made an obscene gesture. "I think that might be your problem."

I grabbed her hand and pushed it to the table, making her wobble on her heels. "Sit down before you fall down. How many of these have you had?"

She held up her hand and raised one finger, then snapped it to two. She looked at her drink, the one I'd drunk half of, and bent her second finger down. Grace was well on her way to a terrible Tuesday of regret.

"I read an article this week that said orphans have trouble finding a significant other when they grow up." She shrugged in a noncommittal way that meant, *I don't know if it's true or not.*

"Well, lucky for me, I have Grams." I'd been living with her since the day my parents died in a car crash. I rubbed the area on my shoulder where the rebar had lodged. It still ached sometimes, especially when the weather was cold. A constant reminder of a day I couldn't remember. When I closed my eyes, the canvas of my early life was always fuzzy. I heard the screams. I smelled the smoke. I felt my heart race and plummet to a stop. Then, nothing.

I jumped in my seat when my phone rang. The screen lit up while the "Imperial Death March" played.

"Are you going to answer?" Grace picked up my phone and laughed. "Who's Vulture?"

Air rushed out of my mouth in a huff. "Landlord."

She looked down at her phone. "It's the fifth. Didn't you pay your rent?"

I pretended to pound my head against the table. The nearly empty martini glasses shook and jingled.

"Paid what I could."

"Which was?" She raised her hand to Tony again. "Talk of finances requires liquid reinforcement."

"Not enough." I drank martini number two just before Tony brought number three. "I don't want to talk about it." I was down to a blowup mattress and a lawn chair. The only thing I hadn't sold was my computer and my phone—both requirements for work.

"Okay. So, what do you want to talk about?"

I needed to have some fun. "Let's talk about my next date." I looked over the rim of my glass around the bar. People were pairing up now. All it took were a few drinks and a two on the sexy scale to turn into a ten.

Grace scooted around the booth until her back faced the wall. Her green eyes swept the room like laser-guided missiles. "What about him?" She nodded toward the door where three corporate America men stood sipping dark beer.

"Which one?"

"Mr. Tall, Dark, and Dapper." She rimmed her glass with her finger until it sang something akin to a B flat.

I looked at the darkest-haired man in the group. He was fine if you liked trust-fund-babies and country clubs. My tastes were less refined. "He's such a peacock." I preferred a man who demanded respect with a single look while wearing jeans and a T-shirt.

"It's always the birds with you." She leaned over the table as if her sight were failing. After three drinks, maybe it was. "He's more of a rooster, don't you think? I love a rooster's cocksure demeanor—the way they strut their stuff."

"What you like is their cock-a-doodle-doo."

Grace burst out a laugh "That, among other things." She licked the sugared rim of her glass, and I was certain any man looking had just gone weak in the knees.

"What other things?" I barely refrained from rolling my eyes. Grace and I had been inseparable since the day I showed up at St. Mary's dressed in my plaid uniform and my new light-up sneakers. *Sisters from different misters*, but with totally different outlooks.

"I don't know. Handsome in that I've-got-a-Maserati way. And look at his friend."

One guy had a beak for a nose; the other, a barrel for a belly. "Which one? The toucan, or the grouse?"

"I like a man with a strong nose." She looked around the bar again. "Okay, tell me which of these guys is the bird for your nest."

I giggled to myself because anyone coming to my nest would have to embrace simple living and ramen noodles. My eyes went from man to man until I'd rounded the room. "If men were birds, and I had to choose one, it wouldn't be anyone here."

"Oh, come on." She pinched my arm. She had a way of getting the tiniest bit of skin—just enough to send a pulse of pain through every nerve ending. "Play with me."

"I'm serious." I looked at all the pretty boys dressed in Brooks Brothers. "All these guys are birds of paradise. They stand around and look pretty." I drank the rest of my martini. "They don't know what they want. They come here and peck at the feed every night... I want the guy who's not afraid to swoop down and fight for me."

"You're asking for a bird of prey." She bit her lip and raised her brow. "You know they eat everything in their path?"

"Being eaten doesn't sound half bad." I picked up my purse and slid out of the booth. "I'll leave you to your peacocks and roosters. I'll wait for my hawk."

OTHER BOOKS BY KELLY COLLINS

Wilde Love Series

Betting On Him

Betting On Her

Betting On Us

A Wilde Love Collection

The Second Chance Series

Set Free

Set Aside

Set in Stone

Set Up

Set on You

The Second Chance Series Box Set

GET A FREE BOOK.

Go to www.authorkellycollins.com

ABOUT THE AUTHOR

International bestselling author of more than thirty novels, Kelly Collins writes with the intention of keeping love alive. Always a romantic, she blends real-life events with her vivid imagination to create characters and stories that lovers of contemporary romance, new adult, and romantic suspense will return to again and again.

For More Information
www.authorkellycollins.com
kelly@authorkellycollins.com

Printed in Great Britain
by Amazon